SPACE-AGENTS IN DANGER!

'The two agents launched themselves simultaneously at their intended victim. Pias grabbed the man around the waist, twisting him around and unexpectedly off balance. Meanwhile, Yvette grabbed for the blaster in the pirate's belt holster. Pulling it out hilt first, she slammed the hard surface into the weakest point on the man's armour – his faceplate. Yvette made another strike with her impromptu hammer, and this time the plastic broke apart, cutting the man's face to ribbons. She followed up by sending her fist through the opening in the suit. Her punch connected solidly with the pirate's nose, knocking his head back against the hard interior surface of his helmet. His body instantly went limp as he lapsed into unconsciousness. Pias was unarmed – but not helpless. Using as a missile the now-limp body of the pirate they'd attacked, he hurled it the length of the corridor, scattering the pirates at the other end. Then, fearlessly, both he and Yvette leaped forward to press their attack. The buzzing of stun-guns filled the air as the pirates tried to counter this unexpected attack. Despite their quickness, Pias and Yvette could not dodge all the beams at once and, within seconds they were floating unconscious in the middle of the corridor.'

– *The Bloodstar Conspiracy*

Here is the fifth action-packed novel of space intrigue and adventure featuring the amazing Family d'Alembert.

By the same author

The Lensman Series

Triplanetary
First Lensman
Second Stage Lensmen
Grey Lensman
Galactic Patrol
Children of the Lens
Masters of the Vortex

The Skylark Series

The Skylark of Space
Skylark Three
Skylark of Valeron
Skylark DuQuesne

The Family d'Alembert Series (with Stephen Goldin)

The Imperial Stars
Stranglers' Moon
The Clockwork Traitor
Getaway World
Purity Plot
Planet of Treachery
Eclipsing Binaries

Other Novels

Spacehounds of IPC
The Galaxy Primes
Subspace Explorers

E. E. 'DOC' SMITH
with STEPHEN GOLDIN

The Bloodstar
Conspiracy

Volume 5 in *The Family d'Alembert* Series

PANTHER
Granada Publishing

Panther Books
Granada Publishing Ltd
8 Grafton Street, London W1X 3LA

Published by Panther Books 1978, 1980
Reprinted 1984

A Panther UK Original

Copyright © Verna Smith Trestrail 1978

ISBN 0-586-04338-1

Printed and bound in Great Britain by
Collins, Glasgow

Set in Linotype Pilgrim

Dedicated to Stanley and Alix,
despite the case of the missing Froggy.

S.G.

CHAPTER ONE

THE THOUSAND-POINT TEST

The man stood in the darkened room, nervously awaiting the events to come. His compact body, product of a high-gravity world, was clad in a skin-tight bodysuit that allowed maximum freedom of movement. He had spent the past four months preparing for this moment, and now all his acquired knowledge would be put to the ultimate test. For better or worse, the outcome of this trial would affect the rest of his career. His lips were dry, no matter how often he extended his tongue to moisten them.

Suddenly a bright light shone straight into his eyes. Even as he blinked, some instinct told him he was an easy target standing up here in the glare. Without even knowing where he was going, he crouched and sprang forward in the direction of the light. As he did so, he heard the buzzing sound of a stun-gun, but felt none of the effects. Had he remained where he was, the test would have been over the instant it had begun.

Now that he was moving, he realized that his only hope of passing was to remain in motion. There would be more traps ahead to overcome, and he dared not slow down to let them reach him. Safety, he had been taught, lay in speed. But not blind speed; his reflexes had to be in a complete linkage with his brain to achieve the finesse that many delicate situations required. He had to think as he moved, so that thought and deed could be accomplished as close to simultaneously as possible.

He knew of only one thing in this darkness besides himself – the light that was still shining almost directly into his eyes. As long as that light was on him he would be in constant danger. It made sense, therefore, to move toward the light and put it out of commission before the stun-gun's owner put *him* out of commission.

His leap forward brought him down on his right shoulder. He rolled as he'd been taught and came up in a low crouch, prepared to move again. He took a few quick steps to his right, then zigzagged back to his left. The short buzzes of the stunner kept sounding out, proving that he was far from home free; but by keeping his movements in a random pattern, his would-be destroyer was unable to hit him.

The light was much closer now. One more small leap took him to a point just beside it. It turned out to be a small spotlight some thirty centimeters in diameter. Lifting his foot in an arc that would have made a ballet dancer jealous, he gave the bulb a vicious kick. The plastic covering shattered and the light burned out instantly, leaving him once more in a darkness broken only by the blue spot before his eyes – the after image of the spotlight.

The sound of the stunner ceased with the extinguishing of the light. The man on trial moved away from the spotlight once more and paused for a few deep breaths, waiting for the next development to break. He did not have to wait long.

Lights came on all around him – not the blinding glare of a spotlight, but a diffuse glow that illuminated all the surroundings. The man blinked and looked suspiciously around.

To his left, the room he had just traversed in order to reach the spotlight was still dark. Before him was a corridor three meters wide and about forty long; at the far end was a doorway to another room. The walls on either side of the corridor were six meters high – too tall for him to jump over even in this gravity that was forty percent of what he considered normal. There were only two directions in which he could move: either back the way he had come or down this new corridor.

The decision was made for him by a blaster bolt that sizzled the air and burned into the ground at his feet. It came out of the blackness he had just left; flying into the face of that kind of armament when another course presented itself would be tantamount to suicide. Without hesitation, the man chose to proceed down the corridor.

This path was scarcely safe either, though. He had hardly begun to traverse it when he found objects springing up in his way. First a pile of boxes rose from the floor, completely blocking the path. There was no way to go around them, so he began climbing over the pile. To complicate matters still further, light beams seared out at him.

They were intended to stimulate blaster bolts, and the man got the message instantly. There was to be no tarrying in this corridor, either.

His climb became a scramble as he finally reached the top of the pile of boxes. Not standing on ceremony, he jumped down to the ground again, narrowly missing the row of sharp knives that sprang up from the ground just as he leaped. More of the light beams were firing at him, making a realistic crackling sound as they passed by.

He ran at top speed, his eyes surveying the path before him in a series of darting glances. He'd gone nearly ten meters without further incident when he noticed that one patch of flooring was a slightly different color than the rest. In midstride just before he reached it, his back foot kicked out, lifting him in an off-balance leap over the one-meter patch of discoloration. He landed awkwardly on the other side, scrambled to his feet and continued on before the light beams had a chance to zero in on him. In one desperate dash he made it the rest of the way down the corridor and turned to the right through the doorway into the next room.

Without warning he felt the ground go out from under him. As he fell, he hit a body of water with an enormous splash. He submerged for an instant, then came up gasping for air. The water was icy, a cold shock to his tensed nervous system; it left a briny taste on his tongue and stung at his eyes as he tried to look around and get his bearings in this new environment.

The room was dimmer than the corridor had been, but still light enough to see by. The door through which he had entered had slid automatically shut, and the ceiling had lowered to just half a meter above the surface of the water, barely room for him to lift his head out and breathe. The walls were perfectly smooth, without a break or a handhold in them. There was no sign of an exit anywhere.

The man continued treading water as he puzzled out this dilemma. There had to be some way out of here; if it wasn't above water, then it must be below. Taking a deep breath, he dipped below the surface to search for the exit.

The salt water stung at his eyes, so he had to proceed by feel. The room was small, basically a cube three meters on a side and all but filled with water. But the water could not occur here naturally; it had to come in from somewhere. He searched with his fingers for the vent.

There! His hands had been passing over the smooth surface of the walls when suddenly they encountered an empty space. Taking his time to explore the opening fully, he ran his fingers around the edge. The hole was not quite a meter wide and less than half of that high. It would be a tight squeeze, but he could manage to get out of there. He surfaced once more for another gasp of air, then dived and pushed himself through the opening.

At first, this narrow passageway continued level, and he despaired of its going anywhere; but, after a couple of meters, it started sloping upward. Finally his head broke the surface once more and he could breathe sweet, fresh air. Feeling both mentally and physically exhausted, he dragged himself up the ramp onto a dry floor, dreading whatever ordeal might be next in store for him.

There was only one door in the room, twenty meters away; unless he chose to return to the water he would have to go that way. With a sigh he set out – but, though the room was bare of furnishings, it was not as easy to cross as it first appeared.

An ultragrav unit had been planted under the floor, causing a gravity gradient as he approached the door. Where he had emerged from the water the force was only one Earth gravity, but it rose quickly as he moved. Within only a couple of meters it was up to two and a half gravities. That in itself would not have been too bad, because that was the gravitational strength on his own native world; but it went up still further as he progressed. Within another few meters it was up to five gees, and the doorway looked no nearer than it had before.

He felt as though he had a twin brother riding on his back. Coming on top of all his previous exertions, this was an added torture. Keeping his head up was a major effort; moving his limbs was a near miracle. He moved with a relentless determination to reach the portal. Once there, he was sure, the ultragrav would shut off and he would return to Earth standard gravity. He didn't care what other traps might await him there; they couldn't be any worse than this.

Still the gravity increased, and he sank slowly to his knees to crawl forward. Although the floor looked perfectly level, it *felt* uphill all the way.

At seven gravities his eyes were refusing to focus. He continued forward out of habit and willpower, rather than by any conscious plan. Even holding himself up on his hands and knees seemed too much of an effort. He slid down on his belly and pulled himself along. Sometimes he felt he was barely making any progress at all – but he did move forward, however slowly.

After a dozen eons the force on his body suddenly eased. Startled, he looked around and found that he had passed through the doorway into a well-lit room beyond. There were two chairs and a desk there; the desktop was littered with papers. Before him stood his teacher, George Wilson, in uniform, looking down on him with a smile on his face. 'Congratulations,' Wilson said. 'You seem to have made it in relatively one piece.' He extended a hand to the man's prostrate form. 'Would you like some help up?'

'No, thanks. I can manage.' The testee pulled himself shakily to his feet and, at his teacher's nod, walked over to one of the chairs and sat down.

Wilson took the other chair and started shuffling through the papers. 'Now for the evaluation,' he said. 'You didn't do too badly, actually. You made very good time against the spotlight. You were a bit clumsy jumping over the electrified plate in lap two, but results are more important than form in something like that. You were quick to find your way out of the water chamber, and you had the stamina to pull your way through the grav room. Which leaves only...'

And before he had said another word he was pulling a blaster from a concealed holster. He was still smiling, but now the smile seemed cold and heartless. Wilson would have loved nothing better than to direct a blaster beam straight through his student's heart.

Tired though he was, the testee reacted to this new and totally unexpected threat. All through his training, his teachers had warned him against complacency. 'Expect anything at any time,' they told him. 'In our business, you won't go far wrong that way.'

From a totally relaxed position, the testee quickly pushed his chair backwards and slid under the desk. Arching his back upwards, he lifted the entire desk off the floor and slammed it into his instructor. Wilson was prepared for the trouble and knew how to fall. The blaster flew from his hand and landed on the far side of the room. Both men scrambled for it, but the student got there first. Picking up the weapon, he aimed it squarely at his teacher. 'Khorosho,' he said between pants, 'maybe now you'll tell me what's going on.'

In the control center, a host of technicians kept a careful watch on the events of the test, making sure everything started when it should and that nothing, no matter how dangerous it seemed, would cause any serious harm to the participant. The purpose was not to kill him, but to discover exactly what his capabilities were in field action. The Service of the Empire had to know what its agents could do before it sent them out on their assignments. With the safety and security of the entire Empire at stake, it could hardly afford any miscalculations.

Overlooking the rows of technicians monitoring their instruments was a VIP booth, where special visitors could also witness the proceedings. At present there were three very interested spectators: two women and a man.

One of the women was a tall, slender aristocrat with long black hair and a handsome face. Helena von Wilmenhorst was the daughter of, and chief assistant to, the Head of the Service of the Empire. Despite the fact that she was only twenty-one years old, she was rapidly maturing into one of the most capable planners and administrators the Service had ever seen – thanks to the able tutelage of her father. Helena owed her life to the man now being tested, and no power in the Universe would have kept her away from observing his final tests.

The other two people in the booth were similarly indebted to the young man and likewise had a great deal of interest in the outcome. Jules and Yvette d'Alembert, the brother–sister team from the heavy gravity planet DesPlaines, were the top two agents in SOTE's mighty arsenal. Not only were they naturally strong and quick, as people from high-grav worlds tended to be, but they'd had a rigorous training almost from the moment of their births that few people in the Galaxy were privileged to undergo. The d'Alembert family were the owners of, and principal performers in, the Circus of the Galaxy.

In addition to being the top entertainment attraction on any planet it played, the Circus had another attribute: almost since its inception centuries ago, it had been the ultra-top secret right arm of SOTE. Jules and Yvette had been the star aerialists for years before leaving to move up to their true jobs as agents of the Emperor.

They did not look physically imposing. Jules d'Alembert stood only a hundred and seventy-three centimeters tall, though he massed a respectable hundred kilograms; his sister Yvette was ten centimeters shorter and thirty kilos lighter. But the two of them were in a more superb condition, both mentally and physically, than any mere mortal had a right to expect. On the thousand-point test, Jules was the only person living to have scored a perfect thousand. Yvette was only an eyelash behind him at 999.

Now they watched eagerly as their friend, Pias Bavol, went through the final stages of that same test. Although they had met him less than five months ago, the young man had won their friendship and, indeed, saved their lives in a couple of situations on their last assignment. Though he had not had the lifetime background in undercover work that they had, he showed such a proclivity for it that induction into the Service was a logical result. The fact that he and Yvette had fallen in love and were going to be married made it a necessary result as well.

The three spectators watched anxiously on their trivision monitors as Pias Bavol began his ordeal. Each of the three had undergone this on his own, and knew exactly how harrowing it could be. There was no passing or failing mark on the thousand-point test, particularly this final section. Pias Bavol had already done well enough on the written and aptitude tests to qualify for a good job with the Service.

This test, though, would be crucial to his ultimate placement. If he ranked low in field skills, he would be assigned to some less demanding job in administration. Only the select few who could handle themselves well under such arduous conditions could be allowed to undertake field assignments that might put their lives in peril.

Helena laid a hand gently on Yvette's shoulder. 'I hope he makes it,' she said. 'I know you'd like to have him working with you in the field rather than staying at a desk job while you go out on assignments.'

Yvette nodded. 'He'll be smooth, I'm sure. Anyone who could get to Sanctuary and do everything he did without any formal training at all just has to be a natural born field agent.' But her words projected more confidence than she actually felt.

'In a way, I almost hope he doesn't make it,' Jules said softly.

His sister turned to look at him aghast. 'Julie, what a rotten thing to say! Are you jealous?'

Jules smiled at her, defusing her powder keg. 'Damned right I am. You and I are the best team going, and I hate the thought of splitting it up.'

'You mean to tell me you object to teaming up with Vonnie?' Yvette countered.

A dopey grin appeared on Jules's face at the mere thought of his fiancée, Yvonne Roumenier. 'Well, I must admit there will be certain compensations...'

Yvette gave him a triumphant snort. 'I thought as much. But you'd better watch out. Whenever you're with her you keep stumbling over your own feet because you can't look at anything else. Some team you'll make.'

Helena interrupted to bring an end to this good-natured sibling banter. 'It's starting,' she said simply.

Jules and Yvette turned their attentions back to the screens. They watched as Pias Bavol survived his first encounter with the spotlight in the darkened room and then made his way rapidly down the long, treacherous corridor. 'Good!' Yvette called out at one point. 'I knew he'd spot that electrified plate. He's going to make it, Julie, he's going to make it.'

Jules nodded slowly. There'd never been any doubt in his mind about Pias's abilities.

'If he does well enough,' Helena commented, 'my father has a personal gift for you and him, Yvette – two roundtrip tickets to Newforest.'

Yvette turned away from the screen for a moment to stare at her friend open-mouthed. Newforest was Pias's home planet; he was the eldest son of that world's duke. Pias had not been home for close to three years, ever since he had left to seek revenge for the death of his former fiancée. Now Yvette would be returning with him in triumph, to meet his family and share that much more a part of his life. 'Oh Helena, I don't know what to say.'

'Then watch the screen and don't say anything. Father knew how grateful you'd be. It's part of his thanks to you and Pias for saving my life on Sanctuary. And mine too, of course.'

Yvette looked back to the screen, where Pias was now immersed in water and looking for a way out. It was Jules's turn to look at Helena. 'I saved your life, too,' he said with mock jealousy. 'Don't I get any paid vacations?'

'I think Father has something in mind for you – maybe not as much fun, but just as easy. He'll be calling you in to tell you about it tomorrow. Now shut up and let me see how Pias is making out.'

The three young people watched and chortled triumphantly as their friend found his way out through the pipe into the gravity chamber. As he made his tedious way to the exit, all three were groaning in sympathy, shouting encouragement that they knew he could not hear. When he finally made it through the portal, Yvette let out a small cheer. 'Only one more to go,' she whispered. 'Please don't let him be fooled.'

The watched with bated breath as the final scene between Pias and his instructor played itself out. As Pias grabbed the gun and turned it on Wilson, Yvette sagged in her chair with visible relief. Helena leaned forward and punched at a row of buttons in the console before her. Her screen went blank, and a moment later a series of numbers appeared. 'Would you like to see how he made out?' she asked her two friends.

'I'm almost afraid to,' Yvette said – but she looked anyway. There were several rows of numbers on the screen, indicating Pias's scores on separate parts of the test. Yvette ignored those and, instead, checked only the bottom line: 'INTEGRATED SCORE; 994.'

With a whoop of pure joy, Yvette bounded out of her chair and through the door leading downstairs to the evaluation room where she could see her lover again. 'I think we'd better follow after her,' Jules said in a more restrained but still jubilant voice, 'before she hurts herself.' He and Helena left the room at a saner pace, listening to the echoes of Yvette's footsteps leading the way.

Back down in the room, Pias was still holding the gun warily on Wilson. A loudspeaker blared mechanically out of the wall, 'This section of the test is over. Applicant is to proceed to Evaluation Room for final processing.'

Wilson smiled at his student. 'It's over now. Sorry to have to do that to you, but it *is* a necessary part of the test. In our business you can't really trust anyone completely.'

'Then how do I know to trust you now?' Pias was not about to let go of the gun.

'You could try shooting me if you like; the gun doesn't work. I'm just going to stay here while you go through that door. I'm told there'll be someone there who may convince you, although I'm not allowed to see who it is.'

Pias backed carefully to the door, not taking his eyes off the other until he reached it. Then, as a test, he aimed the blaster at the floor and fired. Nothing happened. With a grin, he tossed the blaster lightly back to his teacher. 'Thanks for all you've taught me,' he said.

In reply, Wilson raised his hand in the air in a general salute. 'Here's to tomorrow, fellow and friend,' he said.

'May we both live to see it,' Pias finished the Service toast. Then, without further ado, he turned and went through the door.

Almost immediately he was being smothered by a passionate female form. 'Hey, I thought the test was over,' he protested. 'I didn't know I'd have to risk being kissed to death as well.'

'You're all wet – literally,' Yvette laughed between kisses.

'It's a good thing I love you so much, you sopping specimen of humanity.' She went right back to kissing him and Pias, despite his general fatigue, resigned himself to his fate. If he were going to be kissed, he might as well enjoy it.

CHAPTER TWO

ABELARD THE LIBRARIAN

A less touching encounter was taking place 15,000 kilometers away, on another continent of Earth, in a tastefully decorated suite of offices. The woman who was known to most only as Lady A sat behind a large desk whose top was abnormally tidy. She used the desk largely as a prop, to put more social distance between herself and whoever else was in the room. It gave the impression that she was unapproachable – which was all but true anyway.

Abel Howard, the man she was currently interviewing, seemed unimpressed by the trappings of her office. He was a big man with wide shoulders and a narrow intellect, and he was not accustomed to thinking of women as anything more than kitchen helps or playthings. The fact that he was being hired by one was an anomaly, but he expected the situation to right itself very shortly.

Lady A sized Howard up. She had seen his like many times before; unfortunately, in her line, she frequently had to deal with society's outcasts to accomplish her purpose. She was patient, however; she could wait for the proper moment to assert her authority.

'You say you have ten men at your disposal?' she asked.

'That's right.' Howard leaned his knuckles on the end of her desk like a gorilla – which he resembled in more ways than one. 'You couldn't ask for better.'

'I need a gang with more muscle than that,' she said, a sweet smile spreading across her face. Anyone who knew her would have dreaded that smile. 'Some of the targets you'll be after will be pretty well guarded. I'd suggest at least twice that number.'

'I'll take that under consideration, gospozha, but as far as my gang goes, *I* make the decisions.'

Lady A decided that the insolence had gone far enough. Pushing her chair back, she stood up behind the desk and walked around to the front until she was beside Howard. She came barely up to the big man's shoulders. 'You realize that you came to me highly recommended.'

Howard grinned. 'You won't find better on Earth for any money.'

'So I'm told, which is why I've tolerated your behavior thus far. However, there is a certain natural order of things that must be remembered.' She ran one hand sensuously over the front of Howard's shirt. The man's grin broadened. 'That order is, when I pay the money, *I* make the decisions.'

As she spoke, she suddenly grabbed the front of Howard's shirt and pulled him forward. Her other hand grabbed a fistful of hair and jerked his head back, exposing a wide expanse of throat. Howard gurgled a little for breath at the unexpected attack and tried to struggle; but he found that the grip of this seemingly delicate woman was unbreakable.

'Now listen to me, you blubbering baboon,' Lady A said in cold, measured tones. 'I could break you in half more easily than you could snap a twig – and don't think I haven't been tempted. I will be paying you good money, for which I shall expect decent return without insolence. I will be obeyed without question. Do I make myself understood?'

Howard could barely choke out an answer. 'Yes.'

'And another thing. From now on, you are to address me as "Your Ladyship." Is that clear?'

'Yes, Your Ladyship.'

'Good.' She let go of him suddenly and Howard fell to his knees, gasping for air. Lady A meanwhile walked casually back behind her desk and sat down, waiting for his choking spasm to stop before she continued.

'Now, as I said, you will have twenty men available, though you may not need them all on each assignment. If you have to hire more, that is your concern.'

She took an envelope out of one drawer of the desk. 'Here are the instructions for your first target. You are to burn them immediately after reading them. There is to be no trace left of any connection between us. That's all. You may go now.'

'Yes, Your Ladyship.' And Howard backed out the door bowing, a very changed man.

Lady A smiled. She actually welcomed the chance to have gotten a little hostility out of her system. And sometimes a show of force was necessary to keep the hired help in line.

The Empire's Primary Computer Complex was one of the most incredible feats of engineering ever attempted by man. But enormous problems require equally enormous solutions. In order to govern a realm spread out over more than thirteen hundred worlds, vast amounts of information were needed. The information had to be instantly accessible, conveniently located and readily correlated. It would have to be defended against possible attack from enemies seeking to cripple the Empire by depriving it of the very information it needed to survive. And above all, it had to be accurate.

The complex was built and put into operation a few years before the death of Emperor Stanley Nine. An asteroid twenty-five kilometers in diameter was moved out of its orbit between Mars and Jupiter and put into orbit instead circling the Earth. The interior was hollowed out by a series of carefully calculated nuclear explosions, then lined with lead to prevent later contamination. Inside this immense hollow planetoid was constructed the largest, most efficient computer ever conceived. Teams of experts had designed it to the ultimate in technological sophistication; even now, nearly fifty years after its completion, it was still said that no one man could ever fully understand its workings.

The exterior of the planetoid was bristling with weaponry, all under the control of the computer itself. Should any hostile force attack it, the computer would fight back with the most impressive array of armament humans had ever designed. And if fighting proved impossible, the computer/planetoid was prepared to flee. Its own nuclear engines and subspace drive gave it a superb capacity for flight. Access to the computer facilities was strictly limited, and an applicant could only receive a pass after undergoing a thorough security check, thus safeguarding against sabotage to the computer from the inside. It was said that the Primary Computer Complex was the safest spot in the

Empire – and that included the Imperial Palace.

It was now a week after Pias Bavol had undergone the final part of his thousand-point test. Immediately thereafter, he and Yvette had left for Newforest for a well-deserved vacation. Jules d'Alembert, in the meantime, had been working on another assignment.

No one familiar with the DesPlainian agent would ever have recognized him. His wrinkled, ill-fitting clothes had been padded to make him look twenty kilos fatter than he really was. Skilled makeup had aged him fifteen years; there were puffy, dark circles under his eyes and worry lines on a receding hairline that was really a superb wig. His front teeth were slightly more protruding than usual, and he wore thick, gold-rimmed spectacles. His walk was not the springy, active bounce of a young man in prime physical condition, but instead the slow, shuffling gait of an older man who is undecided where he's going and not even sure he wants to get there.

He stepped forward out of the shuttle that had brought him and a dozen others up to the Complex from Earth, then waited in line patiently to get through the checkpoint. When his turn came he stepped up to the window and offered his ID pass. The clerk took it and put it in the scanner, then began asking the same routine questions he'd asked every day for a week, since Jules had started coming up here. 'Name?'

'Pierre Abelard.'

'Occupation?'

'Librarian.'

'Reason for using computer facilities?'

'Research project 1557-FA-724G.'

Jules's voice was fed through a microphone, and the voiceprint was compared to the 'known' voiceprint of the fictitious Pierre Abelard. When the green light lit up to indicate a match, the clerk inserted Jules's ID pass into a retinascope. 'Look into here, please.'

Jules did as instructed, and the clerk measured his retinal patterns against those on the card. It was another match. 'Smooth, you're cleared through to Checkpoint B-16. Here's your card back. Take the tram to your right.'

Jules took back his card, walked through the gate and

went over to the small automated cart the clerk had indicated. He punched his destination into the cart's control box and sat back as his conveyance carried him to the designated area. As he passed through the enormous corridors he could almost sense the feverish activity being carried on through the Complex all around him. Data were constantly being fed into the memory banks by an army of operators, information on every conceivable subject: rainfall statistics for the planet Belange, birth records for the past month in Sector Twelve, financial reports for the leading industrial firms on the Imperial Stock Exchange, retinal patterns for the latest group of felons exiled to Gastonia – anything and everything that could conceivably be of importance or interest to the Empire was recorded here for posterity. Some early critics of the facility had worried about the invasion of privacy that might stem from the use of this computer, but the sheer volume of data had put an end to those fears. A full crosscheck on any individual was too involved a procedure to be done on a whim. The anonymity of the average individual was assured by the very complexity of the system.

Jules's cart stopped at Checkpoint B-16 as directed, and Jules went through another identification check similar to the first. When he had assured these new people that he was who he claimed to be, a guard escorted him to his study cubicle and locked him in. From now until he signaled to be let out, Jules would be totally alone.

The cubicle was equipped for the basic human needs. A small 'fresher unit stood in one corner and a food dispenser was built into the wall to satisfy his appetites. There was a lounge chair, should he grow tired, and a bookreel viewer mounted on the wall. A small desk served as his work area; from there he could link into the computer and receive information either in display form on a small viewing screen or printed onto bookreel tape for a more permanent record. A decidedly uncomfortable chair went with the desk; Jules wondered briefly why institutional furniture was never designed to accommodate the human body properly.

He sat down at the desk and began his researches. Ever since his and Yvette's adventure on Sanctuary, the top

SOTE command was aware that there was a broad-based conspiracy, previously unsuspected, acting within the Empire. Its goals were not yet known, but that it boded no good for the present regime was an obvious conclusion. One of its highest officers, if not the actual leader, was the mysterious Lady A. This archtraitor knew the identity of the Head of SOTE and seemed to have an excellent working knowledge of the Service's activities. The Service, in turn, knew nothing about her. That situation would have to change.

To maintain utter secrecy, only five people within the Empire's forces were allowed to know of Lady A's existence: The Emperor, the Head, Helena, Jules and Yvette. The information had not even been fed into this computer Jules was now using, lest Lady A's conspiracy had somehow managed to tap into its resources. Only as long as Lady A thought her existence was still unknown to SOTE would the Service have any advantage over her at all.

They were grasping at straws, and the Head admitted it. As long as Lady A knew what SOTE was doing, she could act with relative impunity. They would have to plug the leak, and fast – but to do that, they needed to know more about Lady A herself.

To that end, Jules was going through this elaborate disguise to get information that rightfully should have been his for the asking. The Service would have to get its information in roundabout ways. If they simply ran an identity check on all people who looked like Lady A, it could warn their quarry and spoil the element of surprise. So instead, Jules had to content himself with peripheral glances, hoping to find enough small clues to fill in the larger puzzle.

Their starting base was abysmally small. They knew what Lady A looked like and sounded like from a captured recording of her actions. She was a strikingly beautiful woman of indeterminate age, with a cold voice and an imperious manner. They knew she ranked high in the underground organization, and that she knew the identities of the Head and his Girl Friday and some of SOTE's inner workings. And they knew from her clothing that she kept abreast of the latest fashions at the Imperial Court – which required her presence at Court functions occasionally, since fashion was constantly changing. That was all.

In his cover identity as Pierre Abelard, Jules was ostensibly researching attendance at various Court activities as a function of season and other social factors; in fact, he was poring over all the pictures taken at events, hoping for a glimpse of the elusive Lady A, and then checking guest lists for some clue to her identity.

The search was not very rewarding. After a week, all he had to show for his efforts were a couple of faces off to the side or in one corner that *might* be his quarry. The guest lists themselves were worse than useless because they were invariably incomplete. There were always gate-crashers, or last minute invitees who never made it onto the lists, or people who did not show up and gave their invitations to others at the last moment (without, naturally, notifying their hosts), so that names and faces bore almost no correlation whatsoever to one another.

Jules was getting heartily sick of looking at pictures that produced no positive results. He would almost rather face an army of villains armed with heavy duty blasters than have to look at another dull crowd shot of another senseless party. But he knew that the dull parts came with every job, and that for every second of excitement in the field, there were hours of backup research work at some desk. With a tired sigh, he clicked off the current picture and summoned up the next from the computer's memory.

And suddenly he sat bolt upright. There she was, in a full-face shot. She was far in the background, to be sure, but there was no mistaking the cold beauty of her face, the expression of superiority and self-confidence. He had found that she was definitely on Earth at an official Court function at some time in the recent past.

He crosschecked the date of the picture and groaned. It had been taken four months ago in Bloodstar Hall at the official announcement of the Crown Princess's engagement to Choyen Liu, a mystical young man from the planet Anares. There would be no possible way for him to check the guest list for *that* event; it had, by tradition, been a public gathering, open to all who could come. Most of the attendees were the nobility, who found it easier to wangle

24

their way in; but that did not preclude Lady A from being anyone on the entire planet.

Jules felt very frustrated at having a vital clue handed to him and then snatched away again before he could make anything of it. He recorded the data number of the picture in case he should ever need to refer to it again, then went doggedly on to the next picture.

By the end of the day he had found no new leads and was utterly exhausted. It never failed to amaze him how research work like this could be more tiring than any amount of fighting. Bundling up his notes, he signaled to be let out. Several minutes later a guard came and unlocked his door, and he reversed his path to the shuttle entrance. He waited more than an hour for the next craft down to the Canaveral Spaceport, and from there took a taxi to the shabby apartment where 'Pierre Abelard' made his home.

A coded note had been slipped into his mailbox. Quickly deciphering it, he learned that the Head wanted to see him as soon as possible, top priority. Jules shed his makeup in a hurry – a pleasure, since it itched unmercifully anyway – and left the apartment cloaked in the all-concealing robes of a Delfian. He rushed down to his car – as much as any Delfian can be said to rush – and gunned off into the balmy Florida night.

Jules's car looked like a late sports model Frascati, but there were some crucial differences. As soon as he was out alone on the open highway, he activated a series of switches and his car turned into a small personal jet, taking off rapidly in the direction of Miami and the secret headquarters for all of SOTE.

HQ was located in the skyscraper that also housed the Hall of State for Sector Four – with good reason. The Head of the Service of the Empire was the Grand Duke of Sector Four, Zander von Wilmenhorst himself. From this imposing edifice he was able to control the direction, not only of his own sphere of influence, but also of the multilevel operations of SOTE.

Jules had radioed ahead to let headquarters know he was coming, so his small craft was allowed to fly unchallenged toward the tall building and land without incident on the roof. From there he took a private elevator tube down to the great one's office.

Zander von Wilmenhorst decorated with a certain elegant style. The walls and the beamed ceiling were all paneled with rich brown solentawood, with original oil paintings by the best contemporary artists hanging on two of the walls. The eastern wall was a large picture window looking down on a view of the Atlantic Ocean. Curtains now covered the picture window, though; the Head did not want even the possibility of telephoto pictures being taken of one of his top secret agents. The large solentawood desk was, as usual, covered with reports and papers, all stamped to indicate some degree of urgency. The Shield of Empire was inlaid on the wall behind the desk. And standing beside the desk was the Head of SOTE, Zander von Wilmenhorst.

The Grand Duke of Sector Four was an inconspicuous man, who took great pains to remain that way. He was totally bald and conservatively dressed, of medium height and build, in his late forties. The only sign that there was more than an average brain within that body was his eyes; they had a glowing intelligence that could not be denied. In point of fact, Zander von Wilmenhorst was one of the Emperor's premier policy advisors, and had as much of a hand in shaping interstellar events as the Emperor himself.

The Head greeted Jules warmly and motioned him to have a seat. 'I'm afraid I don't have time tonight to be as sociable as I'd like,' he said. 'With the wedding coming up so soon, there are a billion and one security details that must be taken care of no later than the day before yesterday. Most of them are routine but time-consuming. We've handled worse affairs before. But all of sudden, about five days ago, we were handed an unexpected problem that I don't like the looks of at all.'

He leaned back in his huge chair, lacing the fingers of both hands together behind his neck. 'With Princess Edna the only child of the Emperor, and Heir to the Throne, her marriage in seventeen days will be the biggest social event of the decade. And, as you might expect, the nobility is flocking to Earth in record numbers. Even the most minor barons who can scrape together enough cash are going into hock to come. There are going to be more titles in our hotels than in our libraries.

26

'We expected this, of course, and have been preparing our security precautions for months. What we didn't expect is that someone would be making a determined effort to kill certain select members of the nobility.'

Jules grimaced with the appropriate concern, and after a moment his boss continued. 'One marquis stepped into a sabotaged elevator tube and plummeted twenty-eight stories to his death. A viscountess died in a fire that turns out to have been deliberately set. Those two deaths might have been considered coincidence, but there were three other attacks that were far less subtle – a countess and two dukes were victims of blatant attacks by gangs of thugs who struck, performed their assassinations and got away before we could marshal our forces.

'One possibility we're looking into is the terrorist/ nationalist organizations that, for one reason or another, want their own worlds to break away from the Empire. We've got the local offices checking on that angle, but frankly I don't hold much hope for that explanation. The coordination makes it all suspect. Plus, there's the fact that the victims were all carefully chosen.'

'In what way?'

'Each victim was getting along in years. Each was among the staunchest supporters of the Emperor, above the faintest tint of suspicion, even during the Banion scandal. And each will be succeeded, according to law, by an heir who is, from our point of view, less than satisfactory. One heir is wavering just this side of mental incompetence. One is, by private reports, a drug addict, and another is a public alcoholic. The remaining two are spineless cowards. And, with the possible exception of the drug addict, there is nothing we can do to legally intervene and prevent these people from gaining their inheritances. The Emperor can disentitle anyone he chooses, of course, but to fly in the teeth of the Stanley Doctrine without any hard evidence to back him up would cause serious repercussions. It would cause at least a minor revolt among some lords who count on the Doctrine as a shield against imperial displeasure. If they felt they could no longer be certain of safety there, open warfare might result.'

Jules nodded. The Stanley Doctrine, established two centuries ago by Empress Stanley Three, laid down strict rules for inheritance of titles and division of lands. It legitimized every title now in existence. For the Emperor to set that aside without just cause would make the entire structure of nobility insecure. Revolts had been organized on weaker grounds than that.

'So we're stuck with these new people. Any evidence that they're traitors?'

'None at present. But they're the sort of people who could easily be persuaded to fall in with the wrong company.'

'You suspect, then, that some conspiracy has gotten tired of waiting for the older nobles to die off and has taken advantage of the Princess's wedding to give them a little help?'

'Precisely. For all I know, Lady A herself might be involved.'

'Speaking of her, I can't say I've found anything dramatic on my research assignment, but I did come across one item of interest.' He told the Head about the picture taken at the engagement announcement where Lady A had unmistakably been present.

Zander von Wilmenhorst listened with great attention to the report. When Jules had concluded, the Head was silent for a moment, then nodded. 'Yes, that seems to fit. I'm more inclined now than ever to believe she's mixed up in this business. She showed an obvious interest in the Princess's wedding, which provides us with a tentative tie-in. The murders are the kind of long-range planning her organization seems interested in, too. If I were a gambling man, I'd put a nice sum of money on her being at the bottom of this.'

Jules smiled slightly. What were they all in this organization if not gamblers? Every agent and officer in SOTE had to risk his life and/or reputation on a wild hunch sometime. If that wasn't gambling, he didn't know what was.

The Head stood up and walked around to the front of the desk, standing in front of Jules. He leaned back against the desktop, saying, 'We've done some analyses of likely targets, and we're putting extra guards around the names who came out on top. There's one man, though, whom I'd put on the top of my personal list to be hit – Duke Hanforth of Melenaria. He's an old man, a bit eccentric, but totally devoted to the Empire. His son squanders money on fast women and fast living as though he had inside information the ruble would be devalued tomorrow. No indications that he's dishonest or disloyal, but if his debts grow too madly he'd be easy prey for some blackmailer. Besides, I'd like to keep Hanforth alive for personal reasons – he's a longtime friend.

'I'm assigning you to guard the Duke yourself, in addition to the security team I've already assigned. You can pretend to be his valet or personal servant; Bozhe knows, he can use someone to tidy up after him. Think you can handle that?'

'Sounds simple enough. But is he a real problem?'

The Head laughed. 'The Empire should have more problems like that. You'll like him, believe me. Oh, and I've taken the liberty of assigning you a new partner while Yvette's off on Newforest. Any objections to working with Yvonne Roumenier?'

Jules's eyes lit up with delight. 'I should say not!'

'Good. I was able to send a speedship out for her even before this trouble began – I wanted her on hand just in case. I'm told she'll be arriving at Canaveral in an hour or so – you should just have time to make it before she gets here if you leave right now.'

Jules was eager to get moving, but his formal training kept him rigidly in place. 'If there's nothing else you have for me, sir.'

'Just some good wishes and a little advice.' The Head grew deadly serious for a moment. 'This assignment looks like a milk run compared to your other ones. I'm praying it will be. But I'm assigning someone of your caliber to it because it has the potential to explode in all our faces. Keep the lid on it, Jules.' Then his smile returned. 'Stop in at Wardrobe on the sixty-first floor and pick up some appropriate livery for a valet and a secretary. Then you'd better get going. Vonnie won't like it if you're late.'

CHAPTER THREE

HOMECOMING

The voyage from Earth to Newforest took eight days by cruiser. After being away for nearly three years, Pias had very ambivalent feelings about his return. On the one hand it would feel good to return to his old surroundings and to the bosom of his family once more. On the other, he was very aware of how drastically people and relationships could change during a three-year absence, and he was almost dreading the alterations he would find.

Yvette tried gamely to ease him over the troubled moments by keeping his mind on other things – most particularly herself. The two young lovers were in each other's company almost constantly during the trip. They had known each other for such a comparatively short time that they had two lifetimes of catching up to do. Yvette told Pias about the circus; he was to be a member of the family very soon in any case, and he had been cleared by the Head, so she had no fears at all of letting the secret out. She told him stories of traveling around the Galaxy, giving shows and seeing the sights of hundreds of exotic worlds before she was ten years old. She told him of her father and her training, and the exciting missions she had performed for the Service.

In return, Pias told her about his own upbringing on Newforest. His had been a quiet, backward world, almost primitive in many respects. Newforest had been founded by a dissident group of Tinkers and Gypsies almost at the beginning of interstellar travel, and had kept itself hidden from the empire until fifty years ago. Many of the old customs and traditions were still observed.

As the Duke's oldest child, Pias had been brought up with the concept that one day he would rule this planet. But though his people were settled now at last, some of the Gypsy heritage remained in his blood. Though he never left the planet physically, he read every bookreel he could find about life in the outside universe. He fantasized untold volumes of epics with himself as the hero. But he had no hope that they would ever be fulfilled.

Then a tragedy struck, so terrible that even now, years later, talking about it was painful. Miri, his fiancée, had been killed by a space pirate, in so bloodthirsty a fashion that Pias's soul had cried out for revenge. With his father's blessing, he left his home world and set out across the Galaxy to track down the killer – and, in the process of successfully doing so, his fate had become inextricably entwined with Yvette's. In satisfying his old revenge, he had gained both a new fiancée and a new cause to champion – the security of the Empire itself.

After an uneventful voyage, their ship landed at Garridan Spaceport, and Yvette and Pias debarked. To both of them, the feeling of Newforest's higher gravity – two and a half times that of Earth – was a welcome sensation. Both had been spending too much time of late on lighter gravity worlds; the renewed intensity here had a steadying effect. Walking with firm steps, they descended the passenger ramp and arrived at the Customs checkpoint.

Yvette, feeling very nervous at the prospect of meeting her future in-laws, had chosen her outfit most carefully : a formal turquoise tunic-jacket and a white silk shirt, with matching turquoise slacks and boots. She was bareheaded and wore no jewelry, hoping to give the impression of calm sensibility. Beside her, Pias wore the standard fashion he'd adopted in his travels : a sleeveless chocolate brown jumpsuit with a deep U neckline over a pale orange ruffled shirt. He wore a yellow scarf about his neck and a waist-length brocade cape in swirls of brown, gold and orange. On his head was a broad-brimmed brown hat with an orange rose tucked into the band.

Pias had not messaged ahead to let his family know he was coming; but a sharp-eyed Customs official had spotted his name on the incoming passenger roster and alerted both the family and the news media. As Pias and Yvette walked through the doors, a cheer went up and they suddenly found themselves surrounded by wellwishers.

Yvette watched her fiancé almost vanish beneath a swarm of people that materialized from out of nowhere. Women ranging in age from ten to thirty, all in brightly colored blouses and skirts, were doing their utmost to throw their arms around Pias and smother him with kisses, babbling in the native language that Yvette did not understand. Pias was not struggling noticeably to get away from their grasp.

'I didn't realize you were this popular with the ladies,' Yvette said, letting a trace of good-natured jealousy creep into her voice.

Pias finally made a half-hearted attempt to drag himself out from under the pile of femininity. 'They're all sisters and cousins.'

'Sure they are.'

'Well, maybe a *few* of them are old friends,' he grinned, and Yvette laughed at his embarrassment.

Before all of the women could have their chance to kiss him, however, they were being elbowed aside by an equally friendly group of men, who proceeded to give Pias a series of bear hugs so thorough that Yvette felt sure her fiancé's ribs would feel bruised for a week. They pounded him on the back, kissed his cheeks, laughed and made what were obviously ribald comments about all the things that must have happened to him while he was away. Yvette found herself being pushed very much into the background, but she didn't mind. This was Pias's show, and he should be given the chance to enjoy the spotlight for a while.

One young man held back from the admiring group, and Yvette had the opportunity to give him some attention. He was about the same height as Pias, though with darker, straighter hair, a gold earring in his left earlobe, and a neatly trimmed mustache. There was a brooding melancholy about his eyes, quite the opposite of Pias's normal cheerfulness, but otherwise his features showed a strong similarity to those of her fiancé. From all Pias had told her, Yvette surmised that this must be Pias's younger brother Tas. He was dressed in black coveralls, in stark contrast to the festive apparel of the others.

After several minutes, Pias was finally able to break away from the throng of wellwishers. Taking Yvette by the hand, he led her over to the corner where the young man stood. Pias embraced him, but the other's return embrace was purely perfunctory. As Pias backed away again, he turned to his fiancée and said, in Empirese so Yvette could understand, 'This is my brother Tas. Tas, I'd like you to meet Yvette Dupres from the planet DesPlaines.'

Yvette had warned Pias against giving her real name, even to his family. Officially, 'Yvette d'Alembert' was still starring in the Circus of the Galaxy along with her brother Jules. There had been a 'Jules and Yvette' ever since the Circus had been formed, with new performers taking over the roles every decade or so. The current pair were Yvette's younger cousins, while the older Jules and Yvette were serving as SOTE's top agents. Yvette had not even her name to call her own any more, but she hardly gave that a thought. There was, after all, more to herself than just a name.

Tas Bavol gave her a look that would have made an ice cube shiver. 'Pleased to meet you,' he said in Empirese with cold formality. His voice had a thick accent; he was obviously unused to speaking the Empire's official language, though like most people in the upper classes he had a thorough education in it.

Pias could detect the hostility in his brother's voice, but deliberately ignored it. 'Where's Poppa?' he asked.

'Poppa's ill, very ill,' Tas informed him. 'He's been that way for the past year. All he can talk about is wanting to see his precious Pias again.'

Pias became very concerned at the news, so concerned that he paid little attention to the jealousy exuding from his brother's voice. Yvette noticed it, however, and filed the fact away for future reference. Pias had not told her about any sibling rivalry between himself and his brother, and she wondered exactly what sort of family relationship she was marrying into.

'I must get to him at once,' Pias said. 'Is there a copter ready?'

'Yes, out this way.'

Tas started out a gateway and Pias followed him. As Yvette started after the brothers, a customs guard stopped her. She was a little startled, and Pias had to turn back and tell the guard, 'She's with me.' Only then was Yvette allowed to accompany the two men to the waiting copter.

'Don't worry, darling,' Pias told her. 'I won't let them separate us.' Tas, upon seeing that interchange, grew even colder toward Yvette than he'd been before.

Outside, although it was midday, Yvette was hit by the impression of late afternoon. Newforest's sun was a dim red star, and the illumination it provided was weak at best. There was a slight chill in the air reminiscent of late autumn, though Yvette was not sure what season it actually was. The red sun gave everything a sunset hue.

As the copter lifted into the air, she got her first clear view of Garridan and had to struggle to hide her surprise. Garridan was little more than a town, scattered in a rambling way over a couple dozen square kilometers. There didn't seem to be any buildings over four stories tall, with the vast majority being simple one-story affairs. For the capital city of an entire planet it was remarkably primitive; Yvette had to remind herself of Pias's description of Newforest as a planet where the people still clung to their simpler lifestyle. They'd been out of the mainstream of civilized life for centuries, and only within the last lifetime had they been brought back into contact with the Empire. The entire planet retained the casual, backwater flavor of an outlying province.

The impression that struck her next was of the color. The brown of Newforest's soil mingled with the brilliant red of the native vegetation. Greens and blues were almost non-existent except on some of the buildings – and even then, the red sunlight gave a funny cast to their hues. Newforest, though a gentle place, seemed to be a planet that bathed regularly in blood.

Looking down at her own clothes, Yvette frowned. The turquoise outfit she'd chosen so carefully looked like a washed-out shade of purple in this light, making her seem positively drab in comparison with the other women she'd seen at the spaceport. In addition, local custom seemed to dictate skirts for women rather than slacks, making her feel out of fashion.

By contrast, the lighting made Pias look even more resplendent. The brown of his jumpsuit and hat verged on black, the orange of his shirt and cape flared into red. He had lived most of his life here and knew how to use the lighting to best effect. Yvette found herself wishing she'd at least worn a bright scarf or some flashy jewelry.

Hardly a word was spoken within the copter as the pilot

flew them toward Pias's home. The returning marquis was lost in his concern over his father, and his normally cheerful expression was replaced by a somber one. Occasionally, when he appeared too worried, Yvette would reach out and squeeze his hand reassuringly; Pias would smile at her and, for a moment or two, put his family troubles further back in his mind. Tas, meanwhile, took in every detail with his deepset, glowering eyes. He said nothing, but the emotions smoldering under the surface were more than obvious – and a little worrisome – to Yvette.

After a ten-minute flight, the copter descended toward a spacious estate, well forested. The house, though only two stories tall, was still the largest single building Yvette had seen since her arrival. On any other world, she would have thought it the manor of some prosperous baron or count; but here she correctly guessed it was the ducal home of the reigning family of Newforest. Even the d'Alembert castle on DesPlaines, modest though it was for such a structure, looked regal by comparison.

As the copter landed on a broad lawn in front of the manor, a handful of servants dressed in livery came out to greet them; only the distinctive earrings they wore served notice that they belonged to this particular household. Pias took Yvette's hand and led her over to one of the servants, an older man with gray hair and laugh-wrinkles around his eyes. 'Yuri, this is Yvette,' Pias said in Empirese. 'Take her and her things to the best guest room available and see that she's comfortable. Is my father in his bedroom?'

The servant nodded, and Pias turned to Yvette. 'I have to go see him at once. You understand. Let Yuri make you comfortable, and I'll be back with you as soon as I can. He speaks some Empirese, and you can trust him to answer any questions you have; he's known me all my life and he's the closest friend I have in the Universe.' So saying, he kissed her quickly and raced into the building.

Yuri turned to Yvette and gave her a smile. The man was old – at least in his eighties – and looked like nothing so much as a taller-than-average pixie. His smile and the youthful gleam in his eyes, though, belied his age. Yvette decided on the spot that she liked this man, and that Pias's faith in him had been well earned. She smiled back at him and allowed him to carry her lighter suitcase; she insisted on carrying the heavier one herself. She could feel Tas's eyes focused on the back of her neck as she entered the building, leaving him behind.

What she could see of the inside of the manor was as unprepossessing as the outside. Even the largest of the formal rooms would not have held more than forty or fifty people, and were decorated to give a feeling of homey comfort rather than ducal dignity. There were no ostentatious displays of art or wealth; hand-woven blankets and collections of baskets were the only decorations hanging on the walls, while smoked sausages, braided cloves of garlic, and onions hung anachronistically from the ceiling. The fireplaces in the main rooms looked well-used rather than ornamental, and a slight, pleasant odor of woodsmoke clung to the stone walls. The floors were rough slate, uneven in spots, and she had to constantly watch her step to avoid tripping. Shelves and small niches were filled with odd knickknacks, wooden carvings of animals, and toys.

I've been in grander castles, Yvette decided, *but certainly never in one that made me feel at home more quickly.*

'You know Pias long?' Yuri asked in strained Empirese as they walked.

'Only a few months – not nearly long enough, as far as I'm concerned. I hope to make it a whole lot longer.' She was reluctant to spell out her relationship in more detail. Pias had wanted to keep their engagement quiet until he could tell his father first and get his approval.

Yuri did not seem the prying sort, though. His Empirese was not good, and conversation was a struggle for him. 'He look healthy, despite being away. I only hope situation back here won't cause hurt.'

'Well, it was quite a blow to learn about his father . . .'

'Not what I meant. Well, partly, but are other things, too.'

Yuri threw open a door and led Yvette into a charming bedroom with stone walls and windows that overlooked a tiny garden. A small fireplace was set in one wall. 'This be your room, gospozha. If you need anything, just ring bell-pull there.'

As he turned to go, Yvette caught him by the elbow. 'You

mentioned some problems here at home. Is there anything in particular Pias should know about?'

Yuri stopped and looked her over, sizing her up for trustworthiness much as she had done to him a short while ago. She knew she was being judged for how worthy she was of Yuri's master; the servant would also be taking into account Pias's kissing her before running off to see his father. Finally, Yuri decided to open up slightly and trust her. 'It be his brother. Tas be ... changed since Pias go away. They never got on well; Tas always be a wild one. Pias used to hold him back so there be no problem; but with no Pias these last few years, Tas get even worse.'

The old man shook his head. 'Never did like Tas. Should have be strangled in cradle like changeling.' He looked Yvette straight in the eyes. 'Tell Pias, watch out for Tas; he do no good.' Then, without further ado, the servant turned and left the room. Yvette sat down on the edge of her bed and debated what to make of her future in-laws.

Pias ran down the familiar hallways and bounded up the stairs two at a time to get to his father's bedroom. The door to the room was closed, and there was a nurse seated outside, reading. He looked up at Pias's approach and recognized the young marquis immediately.

'Is he awake? Can I go in?' Pias asked.

'Yes, Your Excellency – yes to both questions.'

'What ... what does he have?'

'Mottle fever, I'm afraid.'

Pias groaned. Mottle fever was a disease peculiar to New-forest. So far as was known it was not contagious, and it was only seldom contracted – but invariably fatal. Its course was unpredictable; the victim might die within months, or he could live on for a decade or more while the disease ravaged his body. But eventually it would kill him.

Thanking the nurse for the information, Pias entered the room. It was dark inside, kept that way because mottle fever affected the eyes, making them ultrasensitive to light. Pias waited inside the door until his eyes adjusted to the lower illumination, then looked around.

The room was very much as he remembered it: hand-woven area rugs covering the hard slate floor; the large ebonwood bureau against the north wall with its mirror in the elaborately carved frame; the portrait of his late mother on the south wall, surrounded by smaller portraits of all the children; and the massive wooden bed directly in front of him, with the richly embroidered canopy and drapes that had so impressed him as a small child.

His father lay on the bed, very still. Duke Kistur Bavol was in his middle sixties. When Pias had left home almost three years earlier, the Duke could have been mistaken for a man in his forties, but now he looked every year of his true age. His hair, which had been light brown, was now a mane of white, and his leathery skin was mottled with the dark patches that gave his disease its name. His eyes, which before had missed nothing, now seemed watery and luster-less.

As Pias stood there silently, not knowing what to say, the old man slowly propped himself up and peered out at him. 'Who's there?' he asked weakly.

'It's me, Poppa. Pias.'

The Duke peered at him with rheumy eyes. His mouth moved, but no sounds came out. Breaking down completely, Pias practically flew across the room and put his arms around his father. The two men wept openly for several minutes before any more could be said. Finally the old man pushed himself slightly back from his son and looked directly into his eyes. 'Did you find him?' he asked.

Pias nodded. 'Yes. Miri has been avenged.'

That was all the information the Duke required. 'Good. Now that you have done what was needed, you are back here where you belong. I need you here with me, Pias.'

Pias felt a sudden chill as he was caught in a storm of conflicting emotions. In order to become engaged to Yvette, he'd had to undergo Service training and swear a loyalty oath to SOTE. He'd vowed to serve the cause of Empire now, and his life was not entirely his own. 'I ... I can't stay here, Poppa.'

The old man looked confused. 'What do you mean? You found the man and avenged our honor. This is your home again.'

'But I can't stay, Poppa. I'll have to be leaving again, very soon.'

'Why? Why must you leave your home, your family? What drives you out?'

'I made a promise.'

'To whom?' The old man was sitting up now, anger creeping into his voice. Some of the old fire was returning, but Pias was not happy at having it directed at him. 'Who is more important to you than your father?'

Pias was about to tell him the truth when he became aware of a third person in the room. Tas had entered quietly behind them while Pias and his father had been talking, and was now a presence lurking in the shadows. The Duke had always been loyal, and Pias would have trusted him with the knowledge that he was working for SOTE; but he had an instinctive distrust of what his brother would do with that same knowledge. Lamely, he merely said, 'I can't tell you now.'

'Maybe it's that *gadji*, that outsider woman he brought with him,' Tas suggested. His voice was pure acid.

Pias repressed an urge to strangle his younger brother. He had meant to bring up the issue of Yvette separately, once he'd managed to convince his father of the rightness of his actions. Now Tas had muddied the water still further – deliberately.

'A *gadji*? And you brought her here?' The Duke was furious. 'Have you deserted your own people entirely, then?'

'Poppa, you taught me everything I know about kindness and hospitality to strangers,' Pias protested. 'And Yvette is . . .'

But he could get no further in his explanation. The old man, in his rage, started in on a coughing fit. His nurse ran in from the hallway and quickly came to the Duke's side. 'I don't know what you said to him,' he told the two younger men, 'but he's not supposed to get upset. You'd both better leave, at once.'

Reluctantly, Pias let the nurse shoo him out, along with Tas. The two men stood alone outside in the hallway, facing each other in appraisal like two wrestlers in a ring. Pias thought of and discarded a dozen different questions before finally asking, 'Why? Why did you hurt him so badly?'

'Me?' Tas laughed strangely. 'You'd better check your pronouns. My only target is you. Welcome home, brother Pias.' Turning quickly, he marched off down the hall, leaving Pias no chance for response.

Pias shook his head. It was true that his father's anger had hurt him – but he knew down deep that it had hurt the Duke even worse to feel betrayed by his oldest son. Pias had a sudden insight into just how much his brother must hate him, if he was willing to torment their father to such depths just to indirectly hurt his brother. He had known Tas was a brat even before he left Newforest; but his younger brother had apparently sunk even lower during Pias's absence.

With a feeling of great sadness, Pias started down the hallway toward his own room. As he passed one open doorway, he heard a sultry female voice say, 'Aren't you even going to say hello, Pias?'

Turning, Pias eyed the speaker. She was a beautiful, dark-skinned woman in her early thirties, with jet black hair flowing smoothly down her back to the waist of her brightly colored skirt. Her eyes had an easy, knowing look about them, and her patchwork blouse was so open down the front that it exposed more cleavage than even the liberal customs of Newforest tolerated.

Despite his worries about his father and brother, Pias forced himself to be cheerful. 'Hello, Gitana. I'd been hoping to see you again. I wasn't sure what to think when you weren't there at the spaceport with everyone else.'

Gitana walked toward him, closing the gap until the two of them were just touching. She put her arms around his waist and said, 'I was hoping to give you a little more private welcome.' Her throaty chuckle left little doubt as to her meaning.

Coming on top of the painful reunion with his father, this new circumstance left Pias even more confused. There had been a time, years ago, when he and Gitana had been very much in love – but that was before he'd fallen in love with, and become engaged to, her sister Miri. Gitana had felt bitter then – and now that her sister was safely dead, she obviously intended to take up where they'd left off.

Pias's love for Yvette, though, made that impossible. Feeling very embarrassed, he said, 'Aren't you even going to ask me whether I found Miri's killer?'

'I assume you did; you said you wouldn't come home again until you'd killed him.' She began kissing him lightly at the base of the neck. 'You're a man of your word. Usually.'

'Usually?' Pias tried gently to extricate himself from Gitana's embrace, but his former lover would not take the hint.

'You once said you'd love me until the end of time itself.'

'That was a long time ago, Gitana. People change, sometimes.'

'I haven't.' Gitana pulled him more tightly to her, and started backing both of them into the room she'd come from. 'I still love you, Pias.'

'But I don't love you.' The words were out of his mouth before he could hold them back.

He could feel Gitana stiffen against his body. Her fingernails dug painfully into his back. 'Who, then? That little simp of a *gadji* I saw you get out of the copter with? Why settle for a thin-blooded little prissyfoot when you can have a *real* woman?'

Yvette's five times the woman you'll ever be, Pias thought, but this time kept the words diplomatically to himself. He'd hurt her badly enough already; there was no need to add to the insult further.

Instead, with a decisive gesture, he pulled away from her and said, 'Gitana, please. We're only hurting ourselves more by dredging up old ghosts and old sorrows. You're a beautiful woman with dozens of men at your feet. I can't be all that special; there are probably plenty of them better for you than I am.'

Gitana backed one step away. Her eyes showed clearly the volcano smoldering within her soul. 'Then you reject me again?'

'It's not a question of rejection ...'

But Gitana was gone, vanished back into the room from

which she'd emerged. The door slammed behind her, a final exclamation point to their conversation.

Pias went back to his old room and found it all in order. He lay down on the bed for half an hour, trying to regroup his thoughts and emotions after the disastrous events of the afternoon. Then he went in search of Yvette.

He found her just as she finished unpacking. She could tell instantly that he was not as happy as he should be on coming home after such a long time, but she said nothing about it. She spoke instead about how nice she thought Yuri was and how pleasant the manor house itself made her feel, waiting for him to open up about his troubles.

Finally he did so, telling her the story of his reunion with his father. He told her of the increased hatred his brother felt for him, and how he seemed determined to turn their father against him. Pias chose, however, not to say anything about the equally disturbing encounter he'd had with Gitana.

Yvette repeated what Yuri had told her about Tas, which only increased Pias's depression. 'I never even got the chance to explain about you,' he moaned. 'All my father knows is that you're a *gadji* – it's a derogatory term for women not of our own people. The sickness must be worse than I thought; my father's always been tradition-bound, but he's at least been openminded about people. I didn't tell you, because I didn't want to worry you, but I knew he would be less than pleased about the engagement at first; I had thought that some gentle persuasion would be able to change his mind. That's why I wanted you to come here and meet him; I was sure that as soon as he got to know you, he'd see how wonderful you are. But now . . .'

He sighed and shrugged his shoulders. 'I don't know. I just don't know anything. It's as though there's been a slow poison at work on his brain, and I suspect its name is Tas.'

Yvette held him gently and did what she could to soothe him until it was time to change for dinner. It turned out that all the clothing she'd brought with her was inappropriate for Newforest society; she settled on a yellow tunic-suit as being the best of the lot. Pias, as always, looked dashing in brown slacks and a flowing shirt that had been hand-embroidered for him by his late mother.

Yvette wanted to enter the dining room arm in arm with him, but Pias thought it might be more diplomatic, considering his father's present feelings, if they did not show too much public affection at once. They walked in side by side and sat down next to one another at the long, crowded table.

A few of the people there were quite friendly. Pias introduced Yvette – whom he called his 'friend' – to his sisters. The youngest one, a teenager named Beti, was pleasant and friendly, but two older ones, both married to men Pias had privately described as louts, were stiff and formal. Others at the main table were also relatives, mostly uncles and aunts who also served as the Duke's advisors; the family unit was very strong on Newforest, Pias had explained, and nepotism was not only taken for granted, it was expected.

Very few of the other relatives showed Yvette anything more than surface politeness. She guessed that brother Tas had been busily at work poisoning their minds against her before she'd even had a chance to defend herself. Pias's homecoming, which should have been a joyous occasion, was quickly turning into a nightmare.

The chair at the head of the table, where the Duke would normally have sat, was conspicuously empty – and had been, Beti told them, since the old man's illness began. Nevertheless, proper deference was shown to the Duke's place, and every so often a diner would nod his head out of respect toward the empty chair.

Yvette had never felt quite as out of place anywhere as she did here, but she resolved not to show it. Her strong social upbringing in a noble family enabled her to ignore the slights as though they were not there. Still, the knowledge that Pias's family was rejecting her hurt considerably. She could only begin to imagine what it was doing to Pias.

They were almost finished with the meal when a beautiful dark woman seated down near the end of the table stood up and glared at Yvette. 'I challenge the presence of this *gadji* in our midst,' she said.

There was a muffled gasp down the long table as the

43

various diners reacted to the statement. Beside her, Yvette could see Pias struggling to remain calm as he said, 'Gitana, stop making a fool of yourself.'

Gitana now looked at him. 'I claim you, Pias. I claim you by the oaths you took many years ago and by the fact that you were my sister's fiancé.'

She then looked straight back at Yvette. 'Is there any real woman who would dispute my claim?'

Yvette refused to be daunted. With an expression of supreme calm, she said softly, 'Pias is a free human being. He chooses his own consorts. No one has the right to claim him for anything.'

'Stay out of this, Eve,' Pias whispered. 'Traditions are different here. You'll only make things worse.'

Yvette's words had already inflamed Gitana beyond the point of reason. 'Who is this *gadji* who seeks to instruct me? Am I not daughter of Stiggur, of a noble line and lineage? Am I not of the chosen family for Pias Bavol's mate? Would she deny me my rights by all our ancient customs?'

With a quick flick of her wrist, Gitana sent a dagger hurtling through the air at Yvette. The female SOTE agent gauged its flight path with an experienced aerialist's eye, and did not twitch a muscle as the dagger landed mere centimeters from her hand and sheathed itself in the tabletop.

'If she insults me thus, let her back up her words with actions,' Gitana raged. She had another blade in her hand, and was in a fighter's crouch.

Yvette was taken aback by this sudden turn of events. She didn't know much about who this Gitana was, but she was being placed in a position of fighting for the man she wanted. From Gitana's pose, she was obviously skilled at fighting with knives – and she was deadly serious about this duel.

CHAPTER FOUR

THE DUKE OF MELENARIA

After leaving headquarters, Jules raced his car as fast as the laws would permit to the Canaveral Spaceport to meet his darling Vonnie. Even so he was ten minutes late for the appointed time; fortunately, the ship's arrival was even later, and she was not left standing around to wait for him.

When finally she did emerge from the Customs checkpoint, he ran over to her and they embraced like any ordinary pair of long-separated lovers. They had not seen each other since their assignment together protecting Princess Edna on Ansegria nearly seven months before. They had each stored up a great deal of emotion during that interval and, in the first few minutes, they almost completely forgot they were in a public place.

After a while, however, sanity returned, and Jules pulled back a step to look her over once more. Yvonne Roumenier was same height as himself, with brown hair, almond-shaped eyes, an exquisitely beautiful face and a figure that matched it. Like him, she was also a DesPlainian, and also the child of a noble family – her father, Ebert Roumenier, was the baron of Nouveau Calais, one of the most important cities on DesPlaines. As the oldest child, she stood to inherit his title one day.

But it was neither her lineage nor her beauty nor the fact that she was engaged to Jules d'Alembert that had led the Head to choose her for this assignment. Yvonne Roumenier had scored 989 on the thousand-point test, making her one of the most capable agents at his disposal. The fact that she and Jules made such a compatible team was at most a secondary consideration.

'I could stand here looking at you all day,' Jules said at last, 'but we've got an assignment that we should be on as soon as possible – meaning ten minutes ago.'

'Before I even get a chance to unpack?' Vonnie asked. She was still a little breathless from Jules's kisses, and was unprepared for such a rush.

'Relax, that's part of the assignment. We're live-in bodyguards for Duke Hanforth of Melenaria, so we go straight to our assignment and check in there. I've already got a uniform for you – you can change in back while I'm driving.'

Jules took her suitcases out to his car and packed them neatly in the back. As they drove to the outskirts of town, Jules explained as much of the Head's theories as Vonnie needed to know – that someone seemed to be in the assassination business, and that Duke Hanforth appeared to be the next prime target. The two of them were being assigned as personal servants to the Duke in addition to a regular SOTE team of security agents; the regulars would not know Jules and Vonnie were on their side, for the security of all concerned.

Once out in the open countryside, Jules converted his car once more into an aircraft, and the two of them began zooming through the uppermost reaches of the atmosphere toward the Angeles–Diego complex where Duke Hanforth would be staying. The journey took them all night, but they hardly minded that – they had a lot of news to catch up on, and a lot of stored up love to express, now that they were alone. In those spare moments between kisses, Jules told Vonnie about Yvette's new fiancé, and Vonnie was delighted at the news. 'Maybe we can have a double wedding ceremony,' she exclaimed.

The arrived in Angeles–Diego just after sunrise the next day. Jules drove to the Luxoria Hotel, where the Duke was supposed to be registered, but he was in for a bit of a surprise when he inquired at the front desk.

'No, that old windsucker isn't here,' the clerk snorted, 'and I'm just as glad. He called our hotel a chrome-plated rubbish heap.'

'Why did he do that?' Vonnie asked.

'Because we didn't have any accommodations for him on the ground floor, and he hates elevator tubes, that's why. Said it was bad enough he had to travel in a metal boxcar all the way from Melenaria and a flying lawnmower from the spaceport to here; he didn't want to have to ride on magic carpets just to get to and from his room.' The clerk sniffed as though his personal honor had been assaulted.

'Do you know where he *is* staying, then?' Jules asked, becoming a little concerned about finding the man he was

46

supposed to guard before anything could happen to him.

'Someplace without an elevator tube, obviously. Probably without even running water, if he has his way. It's crazy old blots like him that make you question the rationale for hereditary aristocracy.' The clerk turned away and refused to say any more to them.

Jules and Vonnie spent the next two and a half hours calling all around Angeles–Diego trying to locate their wayward duke. Finally Vonnie contacted a rental agent who had leased the Duke a private villa near the ocean at Malibu – a sprawling one-story estate surrounded by lush gardens, and probably costing five times what the Duke would have spent for the most elegant suite at the Luxoria.

'Well,' Jules shrugged, 'the Head warned me our duke was an eccentric sort; I guess we're finding out just how eccentric he is.'

They drove to the address the rental agent had given them and were challenged at the gate by the regular SOTE people, who had already managed to find and attach themselves to the man they were protecting. Jules showed the phoney ID cards he'd been given, establishing himself and Vonnie as Fedor and Karolina Khermikov from the Star Lane Temporary Employment Agency. Fedor was hired to be the Duke's valet while the old man was visiting Earth; Karolina was to be his personal secretary. Both of them were given a thorough screening before they were allowed to pass through the gate and go to the house itself.

The beautiful exterior of the house – well worth every cent the Duke was paying for it – gave no indication of the chaos the two agents found as they entered. Suitcases and trunks lay scattered about the floor throughout the hallways, making walking difficult. Some had been opened, their contents thrown randomly about as though by a hasty burglar. Articles of clothing lay where they'd been thrown, either on the floor or draped at cockeyed angles across pieces of expensive furniture. Jules and Vonnie exchanged curious glances. Had the house already been broken into, without the knowledge of the guards at the gate?

Just then a figure burst energetically out of one room. He seemed like a scarecrow parody of a man, tall and gangly and constructed of odd-lot pieces. His hair was silvery

47

white and straggled in wisps over the top of his partially bald head. His clothing looked as though he'd dressed in the middle of a rummage sale: the tight pants sported a codpiece more appropriate for a teenager; the sweater was thirty years out of date and trimmed with moldering fur; the shoes were ballet slippers, two sizes too large for the feet they were on. The man moved at a swift pace, though, that belied the look of age about his features.

'Pirates and thieves,' the man ranted. 'I'm surrounded by pirates and thieves.' Then catching sight of Jules and Vonnie, he confronted them. 'Are you here to rob me, too?'

'No,' Jules said, his voice showing the sudden concern he felt. 'Has somebody robbed you?'

'*Everybody* has robbed me! Hotel clerks, restaurant owners, rental agents, cab drivers, porters, bell captains. The entire population of the Earth divides itself into two classes: the pirates and thieves in one class, the fools and incompetents in the other. If you're not pirates and thieves, you must be fools and incompetents.' He gave a brisk nod of his head, as though having just proved an abstruse point of law before a jury.

'I should hope not!' Vonnie exclaimed, to which Jules added, 'You are, I trust, Duke Hanforth?'

'If you trust, young man, you're bound to go astray on this sorry planet.' He moved off quickly to another room, and Vonnie and Jules had to hurry to keep pace with him. 'Yes, I'm Duke Hanforth, for whatever that's worth – and it seems to be worth less every hour I'm alive. Who are you, and how much of my money are you laying claim to?'

The two agents were taken slightly aback by the Duke's brusque manner, but were resolved not to be outdone. 'I'm Fedor Khermikov,' said Jules, equally crisply, 'and this is my wife Karolina. We're here as ...'

'I know, I know. Valet and secretary. As if I'd know what to do with them.'

Jules cleared his throat. 'May I speak confidentially, Your Grace?'

'And how much will *that* cost me?' the Duke harrumphed. 'I've learned that whenever anyone asks to speak to you confidentially, he's out to swindle you.'

'No money involved, Your Grace,' Vonnie said, struggling

hard to maintain her temper in the face of this old man's continuing accusations. 'It's about who we really are. We're...'

'You're special bodyguards from SOTE,' the Duke said contemptuously. 'Young lady, do me the favor of not belaboring the obvious. I was a veteran of political intrigues, before your grandparents even tied the knot – if they ever did. I spent five years as Prime Councilor to Stanley Nine, and I was one of the four people to survive that so-called accident of his.'

Jules was impressed with the Duke's credentials. The accident he referred to was the famous one in which the previous emperor had been killed. He'd been on his way back to Earth after observing some naval training man-euvers, and his private superdreadnaught had materialized from subspace in the exact path of a drifting derelict ship. Before even the deflector screens could be activated, the ship was destroyed, and only four people managed to escape alive – Duke Hanforth among them, apparently. It was a billions-to-one encounter, but SOTE's intensive in-vestigations had proved it was an accident, not an assas-sination – there was simply no way all the possible factors could have been calculated beforehand.

' "So-called"?' Vonnie said. 'Then you don't believe it really was an accident?'

The Duke snorted. 'Nothing is ever an accident, especi-ally where the Stanley family is concerned. I've lived under three Emperors and known most of their relatives – and, with the exception of this current chap, they're the most underhand crew I've ever seen.'

'Yet you served as Prime Councilor for five years?' Vonnie was incredulous. 'Why did you do that, if you dis-liked them so much?'

'Because he was my Emperor.' The Duke drew himself up straight, like an old soldier coming to attention. 'I'd serve a dung-beetle if it were my true Emperor – and believe me, Stanley Nine came close. Hardly a year went by without at least six assassination plots, some barely foiled in time. I don't know who finally did it or how they worked the trick, but there are no accidents around the Stanley family – you mark my words on that.'

He gave another snort and looked at the two of them as though they were paramecia under a microscope. 'And you two DesPlainians are going to keep me safe from this gang that's been murdering nobility, eh?'

'You know about them, then?' Jules asked. As angry as the crusty old man made him, he could not help but be impressed with his intelligence.

'Of course I do. I can read the newsrolls; my eyes haven't gone out on me yet. I can add facts well enough. I may be old, young man, but I'm not stupid. Stupidity's for the young, though I admit they don't hold the monopoly yet. They're working awfully hard at it, though ...'

His voice trailed off and, for a moment, he stared into space at a point somewhere between Jules and Vonnie. Then his mind snapped abruptly back to the present. 'Khorosho, you're supposed to be my valet. Do something to prove it. Groom me into a noble man of leisure if you can – or don't they teach you anything at the Academy but muscle stuff?'

Jules rose to the challenge. 'Your hair's the first thing needing attention,' he said in a businesslike tone, completely ignoring the dare the other had thrown him. 'It wouldn't look *too* bad if it were neatly arranged. Your clothing, however, is another matter entirely. You may have been an imperial advisor, but you have no sartorial taste whatsoever. I expect your entire wardrobe will have to be revised.'

'You would speak that way to a duke, with no trace of respect?'

'No, I would not speak that way to a duke. I would, however, talk to a cantankerous old curmudgeon like that, because I have a feeling that's the only way you'll listen. And as for respect, I trade it in equal quantities only.'

'You.' The Duke turned to Vonnie and poked her in the ribs with one long, bony finger. 'Are you merely a pleasant conglomeration of curves or do you actually have some secretarial skills?'

'Try me, Your Grace.'

'Khorosho, I will. Make a memo to fire my valet – after he saves my life, and not a moment before. Now, are you really married to him, or are you free to fool around?'

'At the moment, Your Grace,' Vonnie said coldly, 'neither.'

'Good. At least you're honest. Let's go.' Duke Hanforth started toward the door.

'Where?' Jules asked.

'You said I needed a new wardrobe. We're going out to buy one. We'll see if your taste is any better than mine.'

He led them at a brisk pace out the front door to the large gray limousine that SOTE had put at his disposal. The driver and bodyguard – both skilled SOTE agents – were lounging about, but snapped to attention the moment the Duke appeared. 'Do you know of any good clothing stores in the area?' he asked the driver.

'The best is Haversham's.' she replied. 'It's about an hour's drive.'

'The whole thing's one big damned conspiracy,' the old man grumbled. 'All of Earth is ruled by the transportation industry. You can't walk anywhere, you can't even get a horsedrawn vehicle if you want one. Nothing but those damned machines. They're starting to take over. I tell you, nothing good will ever come of giving machines too much power.' But despite his objections he climbed into the back seat of the limo, and Jules and Vonnie got in on either side of him.

Duke Hanforth kept up a steady tirade as they drove, enumerating his complaints, real or imagined, against the 'conspiracies' that ran the Earth. When they reached the shop and Jules started picking out a new wardrobe befitting a man of Duke Hanforth's age and station, the Duke found something wrong with every selection. Either he didn't like the color or it didn't feel comfortable or the line was all wrong for him or the material was sleazy or the price was too ludicrous. That last complaint was the one most frequently used, and Jules several times was tempted to say he'd pay the difference out of his own pocket just to get the Duke outfitted properly. He could see now why the Duke's wardrobe was so outrageous; he must have driven all his tailors crazy with his impossible demands.

Finally a compromise was reached that was neither too unacceptable to the Duke nor too outré for Jules's sense of fashion: a set of stylish caftans with fancy embroidery on the sleeves and down the front. The head salesman, with great relief, promised to have the clothes made up to the Duke's measurements and delivered to the villa within two days. That matter settled, the Duke's party left the shop and started the drive back to their villa.

They found, though, that they would have to take a detour because a broken water main had temporarily closed a number of streets. Jules and Vonnie were instantly suspicious of the circumstance, and kept extra alert as they drove.

The car ended up traveling through some of the poorer sections of the city. Buildings were rundown, people wore rags, drunks and drug addicts slept in the gutters. It was not a pretty sight.

Duke Hanforth was oddly silent as they drove through, though his eyes darted back and forth, missing no details. As they drove out of the slum into a more presentable section, Jules and Vonnie relaxed their guard slightly. Then Duke Hanforth spoke up. 'How can they tolerate conditions like that?'

'Most of the people were born there and have lived there all their lives,' Vonnie began.

'I don't mean them. People can live almost anywhere if they have to. I mean the authorities – the baron, count, earl and so forth, all the way up to the Emperor himself. How can they dare to let people under their protection live that way?'

'Earth has a population now of nine billion,' Jules said quietly. 'There is chronic underemployment, starvation, crime. There are relief organizations of various kinds, but the job is so vast and their funds are so limited ...' He shuddered. 'I've seen worse. The planet Chandakha makes what we just saw look like heaven itself.'

The old man snorted. 'Secretary, take a memo. Remind me to donate half a million rubles to these relief agencies.'

'Half a million?' Vonnie was startled. This was a man who had just been haggling over a ten-ruble price difference in clothing.

'*Khorosho*, make it a million then. And twice as much to some agency that will help Chandakha.' Closing his eyes, the old man leaned back in his seat and said not another word all the way back to the villa.

Over the next two days, Jules and Vonnie were constantly amazed at the multiple paradoxes that comprised the Duke of Melenaria. He was old in terms of years and yet, in some of his enthusiasms, he had the spirit and energy of a child. He could be parsimonious to the point of absurdity in his everyday dealings, then suddenly turn around and perform an act of incredible generosity on a grand scale. He saw conspiracies against himself under every bush, and yet was possessed of insight that sometimes made Jules frankly jealous. All these contradictions and more went into making up the extraordinary person who ruled the planet Melenaria.

'I think I like him,' Jules said to Vonnie after their second day on the job. 'Most of the time, that is.'

The attack came suddenly, late at night when all in the house were asleep but the guards at the gate. Had they been ordinary guards without SOTE's special training or equipment, they would have succumbed immediately. But, with the special equipment the Service had provided them, they were able to detect the trouble almost from the onset.

The sweetish smell of tirascaline, a powerful sleep gas, activated alarm circuits in the guardhouse even before it reached a density high enough to affect human beings. The SOTE people were jolted instantly out of their complacency by the sounds of the alarms all over the estate. So quickly were they able to reach for their gas masks that only one guard was overcome by the vapour and left unconscious for several hours.

A large copter descended to the open space in front of the house and immediately disgorged a dozen of the toughest armed killers Abel Howard had been able to find. The men had hoped that their tirascaline attack would incapacitate the opposition enough to make their job simpler, but they came prepared for any eventuality. Clad in battle armor, they immediately drew their blasters and began raying anything that moved.

The guards fired back with blasters of their own. Normal strength weapons would have been almost useless against the armor of the attackers, but these guards were armed with Service heavy-duty specials. A direct hit from one of them could pierce all but the toughest space armor – and these agents were all graduates of the Service Academy with top grades in marksmanship. Although they were slightly outnumbered, they were not to be outfought.

The air in the courtyard sizzled as beams of incalculable energy were traded back and forth by both sides. Where a stray beam hit some vegetation a small fire broke out, and soon there were dozens of them scattered about the grounds. The combatants ignored them; the true danger, they knew, was from each other's weaponry.

After ten minutes of a virtual stalemate, the Duke's 'chauffeur' made a daring move. Filling the beam-proof limousine full of her comrades, she drove recklessly straight at the knot of attackers. As the enemy scrambled out of her way, the doors opened and the SOTE agents flew out, blasters beaming.

What had started as an even contest quickly became a rout. The attackers, realizing their forces had been dispersed, raced back to their copter, their only thoughts now being ones of escape. Three of their number lay dead in the courtyard by the time the rest made it to their craft and started lifting rapidly into the air, but that was as close to safety as they got. A deadly beam from the muzzle of one SOTE agent's gun hit a propeller blade, slicing it off cleanly. The disabled copter crashed to earth again and erupted in a giant ball of flames from which no survivors could be expected.

The instant the alarms went off, Jules and Vonnie were also prepared for action. They came sprinting out of their room, guns at the ready. Their only thought was the protection of the Duke. Along with him they watched the exciting action in the courtyard outside, but they took no part in it. Though Jules was itching for action, he knew that his assignment was to be the last line of defense at Duke Hanforth's side at all times.

It was well that they stayed at their posts, too, for the entire courtyard battle had been just a diversion. While all attention was focused in front of the house, three other assassins crept in through the back entrance. They came boldly, not worrying about the alarms on the back door; there was already so much noise and confusion that no one would be able to notice.

These three assassins were all DesPlainians. Just as people from the d'Alemberts' home world were in demand as body-guards and spies, so criminals from that heavy-grav planet were wanted by the underworld to accomplish a variety of nefarious deeds. DesPlainian malefactors possessed the same attributes of quickness and strength as their more honest compatriots, and they could name their own price for their services.

As the trio of assassins burst into the room, Jules and Vonnie whirled to face them. Jules leaped to one side, knocking Duke Hanforth to the ground just as a blaster beam sliced through the air where he'd been standing an instant previously. Vonnie, meanwhile, had also jumped to avoid a blaster beam, but she had gone straight up. Catching hold of the curtain at the peak of her leap, she clung there looking down on the room as she raised her own weapon into position and fired back.

The assassins had been hoping their sheer speed would gain their objective. Having now lost that element of surprise, they hastily took cover from Vonnie's counter-attack and settled in for what might be, comparatively, a long battle.

Vonnie knew she could not stay where she was; her position was too exposed. With a sharp tug, she pulled the curtain from its fastenings, and both she and the drapes fell once more to the floor. She landed in a crouch, gun in one hand while her other hand still clung to the curtain fabric.

Jules had managed, during the brief interlude, to slide both himself and the Duke behind a solid solentawood table. The heavy wood would not be proof against con-centrated blaster fire, but Jules was not about to allow the three assassins the opportunity to make a concerted attack. Reaching around the side of the table, he fired at their own covered positions.

The explosion of the copter outside startled everyone. The assassins were not sure what to make of it but, like most criminals, they were cowards at base. Such an explosion was not part of any plans that had been developed for this strike. One side or another must have made a decisive maneuver. If it was their side, then more of their own men would be coming in here soon and could take over the job; if it was the defenders, the assassins knew they would soon be greatly outnumbered. In either case, they saw no profit in sticking around here and fighting against other DesPlainians who seemed more than a match for them. Their thoughts turned instantly to flight.

Before they could act on their impulses, though, Vonnie was doing some pretty fancy tricks of her own. Whipping the curtain fabric around her head like an ancient gladiator would whirl his net, she hurled it in the direction of the three killers. The heavy material did not behave precisely as Vonnie had hoped, but the results were satisfactory enough. As it hit its targets, it knocked into them with sufficient impact to push them off their feet and jar the guns loose from their hands.

Jules and Vonnie raced over to the fallen men. They still had their own guns, but were reluctant to use them – not because they felt any sympathy for these hardened criminals but because they both knew that they needed at least one of these assailants left alive if they hoped to gain any further leads to the mastermind behind this plot.

So, instead of simply shooting them while they were down, they launched into a personal attack. Vonnie leaped on one thug, raining a sharp series of blows down on top of him and rendering him almost instantly unconscious. Jules, with the precision of a skilled aerialist, sprang at a second man in a low dive that ended with Jules's head butting into the would-be assassin's solar plexus. That unfortunate wight was out cold even before the air had finished whooshing out of his lungs.

The third man made use of both his own DesPlainian reflexes and the time the SOTE team had devoted to his two friends. By the time Jules and Vonnie had finished with their initial antagonists and whirled to look for him, he had already gotten back up onto his feet and retrieved his blaster. The first target he saw was Vonnie, lying on the ground entangled with the assassin she'd just knocked out.

Without hesitation, the third killer fired directly at her.

Only her equally fast reflexes saved her. Her peripheral vision caught sight of his motion as he raised his arm to shoot, and she acted instinctively. Rolling over on her back, she raised her unconscious antagonist on top of her to act as a shield. The blaster beam hit the hapless foe squarely in the back. The stench of burning flesh seared Vonnie's nostrils, but the bulk of her late enemy's body protected her from the blast.

Even this minuscule delay had given Jules time enough to act. Though he had dropped his gun when he'd butted his head into the man on the ground, he still had his own body - a formidable weapon indeed. Springing quickly to his feet, he leaped at the killer even as the latter was starting to fire at Vonnie. The man tried to swivel and catch Jules in his beam, too, but he was the merest fraction of a second too late. Jules's hundred kilo body rammed into him and the two men went sprawling on the floor.

Had they been fighting in an open area, the outcome would have been a foregone conclusion. But in this room crowded with expensive furniture, Jules happened to come down with his head bumping hard against the leg of a chair. The blow only stunned him momentarily, and against a foe from a light-grav world it would hardly have mattered. But against another DesPlainian it was almost a fatal mishap.

His opponent took perfect advantage of the tiny lapse to extricate himself from the tangle and raise himself up on his knees. He lifted his blaster to fire once more, but before he could do so he was cut down by a beam from across the room. Vonnie had relocated her own weapon and shot the thug before he could fulfill his murderous intent. Then she ran across the room and knelt beside her fiancé. 'Are you all smooth?' she asked.

Jules nodded his head and climbed slowly to his feet. He looked over at the unconscious body of the man he'd butted with his head. 'Well, it looks like we got one alive, at least.'

Then the two of them looked over to the Duke, who stood behind the overturned table where Jules had left him. The old man had a small blaster drawn, and had been covering the entire fight scene, just to make sure it didn't get out of hand. Now that the fight was over, he was tucking the gun safely away again.

'You had that the whole time, didn't you?' Jules exclaimed angrily. 'You could have helped us against those guys, you know.'

'Nonsense,' said the Duke of Melenaria. 'You were the ones being paid to save my life. I wanted to make sure I was getting my money's worth, after all.'

CHAPTER FIVE

THE KRISS

With the blade from the thrown knife still quivering in the tabletop just centimeters from her hand, and with Gitana glaring at her a look that would have scorched lead, Yvette risked a quick glance at Pias. 'What's going on?' she whispered. 'Can she get way with this?'

Pias nodded. 'Unfortunately, by ancient tradition she has the right to duel with anyone who has besmirched her honor or stolen the love of the man she thinks is rightfully hers. As far as I know, that tradition hasn't been invoked in more than a century – but it does exist.'

Gitana was coming nearer, still ranting. 'If the *gadji* sow wants my man, she can have him only over my own bleeding corpse. Or *I* will have him over hers.'

Yvette looked quickly around the table, but was met with looks of stony impassivity. She was not popular here, and no one was about to so much as lift a finger in her behalf. Regardless of whether the tradition was obsolete or not, they sensed that Yvette was somehow a threat to their old-established ways, and they would feel no great loss at her death.

She would have preferred to avoid this fight. She had no real complaint against this Gitana, whoever she was, and Yvette risked her life often enough in the service of her Emperor not to feel the need to test herself in private grudge matches. But there were other factors involved here – and her beloved Pias was chief among them. Although she was not certain of all the social ramifications, she knew that backing down here would shame not only herself but Pias in the eyes of his family and friends. This homecoming had already been enough of a disaster for him; she didn't want to add to it.

Grabbing the hilt of the knife from the tabletop, she pulled the blade free and stood up from her place. 'I don't like fighting,' she said evenly. 'But I *will* fight to protect me and mine.'

In front of her, Gitana gave a smug grin. Behind her, Yvette could detect Pias's anguish. He obviously didn't want her to fight any more than she did – but, like her, he recognized the necessity for this match. 'Be careful, Eve,' he whispered. 'She's good.'

Yvette had already surmised that simply from the manner in which Gitana moved as she approached. Her blade was held point upward for a quick slash or jab, her stance was a slight crouch that would let her spring quickly forward or to either side, depending on circumstance. Her gaze was fixed squarely on Yvette; she would let nothing distract her from her goal of victory. Yvette was not surprised to see these signs of expertise; it only stood to reason that Gitana would challenge her opponent to a form of combat in which she herself was an expert. *It's known as hedging your bets,* Yvette thought cynically.

Yvette moved away from the table toward an open area of the room where she'd have more space to maneuver. Gitana turned slightly and continued coming after her. Around them, the room had grown deathly quiet in anticipation of the blood sport about to ensue.

The two women circled one another warily, spiraling inward toward the center of a small imaginary circle. Each was looking for some weakness in the other's defense, and each was having a hard time finding one. Yvette was patient, however; she hadn't wanted to have this fight, anyway. She could afford to wait all night if necessary for the right moment to move, and she refused to strike first.

Gitana was not blessed with her opponent's patience. After circling for almost two minutes, she grew tired of the waiting game and decided to force Yvette's hand. With a sudden lunge, her knife lashed out at the DesPlainian's eyes.

Yvette was ready for the move. She had sensed the tiny muscle tensions that preceded the strike, and could predict almost the instant it would come. As Gitana's blade came sweeping toward her face, she took a slight step back with her right foot and lifted her left arm to block her opponent's motion.

Gitana's move, though, was a feint; even as Yvette was reacting to the supposed threat to her eyes, Gitana's hand was drawing back and her left leg was lifting for a vicious kick to Yvette's midsection. Not even Yvette's reflexes were fast enough to completely ward off the effects of the blow;

the best she could do was start to fall backwards as she saw the foot approach. The kick did not land as hard as Gitana had intended, but it did have enough force behind it to knock Yvette to the floor.

On a high-gravity world like Newforest, with a surface gravity two and a half times that of Earth, any fall was a serious accident. Even ten or twenty generations had not completely acclimated the inhabitants to such brutal conditions. While their bones were thicker and, to some extent, tougher, they were still basically the same calcium compounds that had evolved over millions of years on Earth. They could – and did – still break when allowed to fall victim to the crushing force of high-grav.

The only thing that kept the fight from being over then and there was Yvette's circus training. Gitana's kick had pushed her off balance. There was no way to prevent her impending fall from happening, but she did know ways to keep it from being disastrous. Using her skills as an accomplished acrobat, she tucked her body up in a compact ball that allowed her to land on the softer portions of her anatomy, cushioning the impact on her more fragile bones. At the same time, she utilized the momentum imparted to her by Gitana's kick to let her roll backward. In one fluid motion she had fallen, rolled and sprung to her feet again, prepared to do battle once more.

I've been underestimating her and overestimating myself, Yvette criticized severely. *I've been so used to working on low-grav worlds these past few years, and so used to fighting people whose reflexes aren't as fast as my own, that coming back to a high-grav planet needs more of an adjustment. Gitana has lived in high-grav all her life, and she's more used to it right now than I am. Her reflexes are every bit as fast as mine. I'll have to watch that.*

The only advantage she could count on now, she knew, was her extra training as a circus performer and her greater experience in life-or-death situations. There was much to be said in favor of such experience, but it could not completely compensate for overconfidence.

Gitana was upset that her trick had not worked. The feint and kick was the prime tactic in her repertoire, and she had hoped to use it to end this fight quickly. Now they were in for a more protracted battle. Gitana was still confident of her ability to win, but she had gained at least a slight measure of respect for her antagonist.

She made another feint, but this time Yvette did not respond to it. Gitana pulled back, and the two women began circling one another again. Yvette felt a little more secure now; having analyzed her opponent, she knew that the other's major weakness was her impatience. She wanted to make something happen fast – and that, Yvette knew, could be her undoing. Things would happen quickly enough, to be sure; but it would be a calculated quickness on Yvette's part, not a quickness born of impetuosity.

Gitana made a slight body fake with her left shoulder, then lunged savagely into an attack. It was no feint this time; her knife was slashing for real as her hand ripped downward in a sweeping motion.

But Yvette was no longer there. She had moved into the fake instead of away from it, so that her body was closer than Gitana had anticipated it would be. Yvette came up under the slashing arm, knife at the ready. Gitana, her own reflexes lightning quick, pulled quickly away – but not quickly enough. Yvette's blade raked the side of her arm, leaving a gash fifteen centimeters long and drawing blood.

Gitana howled with the pain and pulled rapidly away from the encounter. The wound seemed only to have doubled her determination to kill Yvette; she glared at the DesPlainian with intensified ferocity. *Let her get angry*, Yvette thought coldly. *The madder she is, the more impatient and careless she'll become – all the better for me.*

The Newforester made another lunge, which Yvette easily sidestepped. As Gitana came rushing by, Yvette gave her a blow to the back of the head with her right fist, causing her foe to stumble into one wall a few meters away. Gitana's apparent clumsiness invoked a couple of quiet laughs from the audience. They were quickly hushed, but they had reached Gitana's ears and infuriated her still further. She would not be humiliated this way.

Gitana regained her balance and started what seemed like another blind charge at Yvette. The latter was all prepared to sidestep once more but, at the last moment, she saw Gitana flip her knife expertly from right to left hand. *She's ambidextrous!* Yvette thought – and that thought in itself was almost too late.

She had been set to move one way to avoid the knife, and suddenly it was coming at her from another angle altogether. She barely had time to pull her head back as Gitana'a blade slashed for her throat. The point just did nick the skin, and a drop of red appeared.

Yvette, off balance once more, reached out and grabbed the other woman's arm as it went past. This accomplished two purposes: it helped steady Yvette to prevent her from falling again and, at the same time, it yanked Gitana slightly off her stride. Yvette, with the unbreakable grip of a star aerialist, held Gitana and, planting her feet, began to swing the Newforester around her in a circle. Within another few seconds, Yvette was able to grab Gitana'a other wrist as well and began applying as much of her strength as she could to the pressure point there. Gitana felt herself caught between two needs – the need to retain her balance against Yvette's whirling her around and the need to hold onto her knife despite the pain in her hand from Yvette's vise-like grip. It was her attempt to do both at once that proved her undoing. Yanking her arms in toward her body, she tried to break free of Yvette's grasp. But Yvette would not let go and, instead, Gitana's struggles only made her knife slip accidentally from her hand. She groaned and tried to grab for it, but once again Yvette proved quicker.

The instant she saw the knife begin to fall, Yvette released Gitana's right hand and transferred her hold, instead, to the other's throat. As her arm clamped around the Newforester's neck in an elbow lock, she pulled backward, lifting her opponent completely off the ground and thus depriving her of a badly needed leverage point. Gitana began gagging, but as Yvette put her own knife to the other woman's throat even that sound stopped. The room was totally silent at her unexpected victory.

'I suppose, under whatever rules govern these things, that I have the right to kill you,' Yvette said, loudly enough for everyone to hear. 'I certainly have no great motivation to spare you. You attacked me without provocation, and I have every right to defend myself.'

'However,' she went on, 'as far as I can determine, your

main reason for attacking me was that you love Pias – or think you do. In all fairness, I don't think that should be a capital offense – I'm guilty of it myself, after all. You're just a little more demonstrative about it than most. So I'll make you a deal. I'll spare your life if, in return, you'll promise to relinquish to me any and all claim you have held on Pias. Do I have your word on that?' To emphasize her point, she took Gitana's left arm and gave it an extra hard twist behind the Newforester's back. As Gitana winced, Yvette whispered privately in her ear, 'If you don't agree, I'll snap it off right here and now.'

'Yes,' Gitana said through gritted teeth. 'You have my word.'

Yvette relaxed her grip and pushed the other woman slightly away from her. 'Thank you, Gitana. I appreciate that.'

Then she gazed around the rest of the room, looking over a sea of unreadable faces. 'I believe I've had enough of this delicious meal,' she said calmly. 'And I'm afraid all this exercise has tired me out. If you don't mind, I'd like to excuse myself and get some rest.'

'I'll go with you and show you the way in case you've forgotten,' Pias said quickly. Taking her arm, he escorted her out the door, turning his back on the anger and hostility raging within his family.

Later that evening, Tas Bavol knocked on Gitana's door, and let himself in without even waiting for an invitation. Gitana was lying face down on her bed, crying. A bandage had been wrapped around the knife gash Yvette had made on her arm. As Tas entered, she looked up and wiped at her eyes in an effort to hide her misery. 'What do *you* want?' she asked bitterly.

'A few words about our common problem.'

'You mean the *gadji*?' Gitana propped herself up on the elbow of her good arm to look at him better.

'In part,' Tas agreed. 'But she's only a portion of a larger problem – namely, what we're going to do about Pias.'

'He's no longer my concern,' Gitana said, rolling petulantly onto her back and staring up at the ceiling. 'You heard me tonight – I relinquished all claim to him.'

'You're still a Newforester, aren't you?'

'I'm beginning to wonder if I'm anything at all.'

Tas sat down on the edge of the bed, grabbed her by the shoulders and started shaking her. 'My father has mottle fever. He could die at any time. By law, then, Pias would be our duke. He's already told my father he doesn't want to stay here; he's perfectly willing to betray our world and our people for something he refuses to explain. Is that the sort of man you want as your ruler?'

Gitana sniffed back the remainder of her tears as she considered what Tas was saying. Pias had already betrayed her twice – once by dropping her in favor of her younger sister, and now by taking up with this loathsome *gadji*. No, she realized, she did not want him to become the next duke of Newforest.

'What did you have in mind?' she asked Tas.

'We'll call for a *kriss*. Surely there are enough grounds for that.' Gitana looked a bit uncertain, so Tas pressed on quickly.

'If I called one, no one would listen. My feelings about him are well known – besides, I'm next in line. I would stand to inherit if the decision goes against him. Obvious bias. But your father is the most influential marquis on the planet. If you could persuade him to call for the *kriss*, they'd all listen. They'd all come. Once they hear everything Pias has done, they're sure to vote against him.'

'Yes,' Gitana whispered, staring up at the ceiling. 'Yes, that would serve him right, the *neringo*. I'll call my father first thing in the morning. I'm sure he'll be as shocked at all of this as I am.'

Tas began stroking her cheek gently with two fingers. 'And once I'm confirmed as the new marquis and future duke,' he said softly, looking directly into her eyes, 'I could make you the future duchess.'

It took a moment for the full implication of his words to sink into her misery-numbed mind. Then she looked more closely at his face. He was not Pias, but the family resemblance was strong. He was far from unattractive, and if she squinted long enough she could forget the slight differences...

Tas bent over to kiss her. She knew one slight moment of further uncertainty, then gave herself in to the situation. Reaching her arms up around his shoulders, she pulled him down on top of her and returned the kiss with all the frustrated passion she had felt for his brother.

The next day Pias and Yvette strove hard to put all the unpleasantness of the past twenty-four hours out of their minds. They stayed completely away from the rest of the Bavol family, hoping that events would be forgotten and that the anger and resentment would cool in their absence. It was a forlorn hope, and both knew it, but neither said a word about it.

During the morning, Pias showed Yvette around the estate, with a special tour of the elaborate gardens. Yvette was fascinated by all the redness of the vegetation. Because the radiation curve from Newforest's sun peaked in the infrared portion of the spectrum, the local variety of chlorophyl – which allowed the native plants to use this light as their food and energy source – reflected light at a lower frequency. It seemed strange at first to see so many multi-colored flowers atop red stems and sprouting red leaves, but Yvette had seen many strange sights in her travels around the Galaxy so far, and quickly accustomed herself to it. Pias took great delight in naming all the flowers and explaining to her some of their peculiar characteristics.

'The red color is one of the main reasons why I love Earth roses so much,' he explained. While he had been traveling through the Empire on his quest, he had made it his custom to wear a fresh red rose every day, either in his hat brim or on his sleeve. 'It's something unmistakably Earthly, and yet its color captures the quintessence of my own home planet. I once tried to have the gardeners plant rose bushes here in our garden, but the gravity and the strange sunlight were too much for them and they never grew properly.' He sighed wistfully. 'Things I love just don't seem to transplant well to Newforest.' And then he

66

changed the subject abruptly.

After consuming the delightful picnic lunch Yuri had packed for them, Pias took Yvette into the capital city of Garridan for an afternoon of shopping and sightseeing. There were no museums or architectural wonders to visit, but Yvette took immense interest in seeing the shops of the local craftsmen. Newforest was still so sparsely settled a world that it had no heavy industry; virtually all the local goods were hand made. Yvette spent a fascinating hour watching a glassblower work at her trade. She visited the local weavers and admired their cloth and rugs. A potter offered to give her a free lesson in ceramics, and Yvette sculpted a slightly off-kilter pot; the man nodded politely to her, but Yvette was sure he would probably remold it once she had left. She had spent so much time on the more populated, more progressive planets that she had forgotten how much tranquility could exist on the simpler ones.

Pias was recognized everywhere they went. Word of his return had spread throughout the city, and everyone seemed to greet him like a long-lost relative. If there had been any news of trouble among the Duke's family, it had not filtered down to the populace. The ordinary people of Newforest loved Pias, even if his relatives did not.

The pair returned to the Bavol manor to find a large number of private copters sitting in the front courtyard. Pias recognized most of the heraldic devices on the sides which marked the vehicles as belonging to some of the most important nobles on the planet. Perhaps at that moment he had some notion of what was about to happen; but if the idea crossed his mind, he kept it entirely to himself. Yvette, too, noted the abundance of nobility, but she resolved not to say anything unless Pias first brought the subject up.

They had their dinner privately, alone together in Pias's room, and as they ate they could hear the arrival of still more copters. Pias began feeling very jittery. After dinner he showed off his collection of bookreels, but his eyes kept wandering to the door, as though expecting someone to come at any moment.

Finally his fears were confirmed. Two of his uncles came into the room without knocking and stood to either side of

the doorway. 'Pias Bavol,' one said, 'you are summoned to the *kriss*.'

Pias gave a slight shudder, then closed his eyes and nodded slowly. '*Khorosho*, I'll be down in a few minutes.'

'You'll come with us *now*.'

Pias looked for a moment as though he'd explode with anger; then suddenly that look vanished, to be replaced by an expression of resignation. As he started to walk toward his two uncles, Yvette grabbed his arm.

'What's the *kriss*?' she asked.

'It means "the law". It's a throwback to the old tribal system of justice, where the elders – or, in the present case, the nobles – sit in judgment of some offender. It's a trial for the violation of tribal tradition.'

'But what have you done that's so wrong?' Yvette persisted. She looked at the two men standing by the door, but they gave her no indication.

'I'm not precisely sure, though I can make a few guesses. Tas will come up with some interesting charges, I'm sure – I can see his not-so-subtle hand behind all of this.'

As he again moved toward the door, Yvette said, 'Let me come with you. This is partly because of me, I know it...'

Pias shook his head. 'The *kriss* is for men only – another old tribal throwback. And even if women were allowed, they'd still bar you – you're a stranger, an outsider, and therefore unwelcome. This is something I have to face for myself. Wait here for me.'

Yvette wanted to ask him what this tribunal could do to him if it decided against him; but he and his two uncles were out the door so quickly that the question died unborn on her lips. It couldn't be too bad or he would have put up a fight, she was sure of that. So the only thing left for her was to do as he'd suggested – wait here for his return.

Minutes dragged by for her like years. She tried to interest herself in one of Pias's bookreels, but none of them seemed worthwhile at the moment. She paced the room, staring out the window at the darkness beyond and trying to make sense out of everything that had happened since she and Pias had arrived on Newforest. She wished she were fighting ten of Lady A's most ferocious minions – anything seemed preferable to facing this unmitigated torture.

The upper floor of the house seemed deserted. Every time a board creaked or the house made some minor settling noise she would jump up and run to the door hoping to see her fiancé returning. All of her finely tuned senses were on alert, awaiting some sign that he was coming back to her unharmed.

An hour passed, then two. Were there loud noises downstairs, the sounds of an argument? Yvette could not tell; her imagination was afire, and every slight stirring only served to feed the flames. She tried to picture Pias standing before the *kriss*, arguing against his brother. How would he do it? Would he be defiant or contrite? Sincere or flippant? Would the confrontation devolve to a knife fight as had her duel with Gitana? Or would it remain a verbal duel only? Over and over, her unasked question returned to her mind: what could they do to him if they found him guilty of some violation? Could they kill him? And how many of them would she kill if they did?

At last she heard the sound of footsteps coming down the hall at a rapid pace, a pace that connoted violent emotions. She tensed, preparing herself for instant action should any enemy come through the door. She was not a part of their barbaric system, and she certainly wouldn't give in to them without a fight.

The door flew open and Pias stormed in. His face held an expression of anger she would have thought totally alien to his normally happy-go-lucky personality. 'The little bastard,' he muttered. 'The drapping little . . .'

'What happened?' Yvette asked, crossing the room quickly to stand by his side.

Pias smacked his palm with his fist and seemed for a moment not to have heard her. 'I never would have thought so much cruelty could exist in one spot!' He looked at Yvette as though seeing her for the first time. 'Do you know what that younger brother of mine did?'

'No. That's why I asked you.'

Her calm voice took some of the edge off his anger. He put his hands on her shoulders and she could feel him still trembling with rage. He stopped for a moment and tried to organize his thoughts. 'My father, as duke, had to preside over the *kriss*. They brought him down from his sickbed especially for the occasion. I don't mind anything Tas can do to me, he's always been a brat. But taking my father apart in public like that ... *our* father ...'

He took a deep breath and tried to calm down. 'I was accused,' he said in more level tones, 'of betraying my people. Tas told them that, while I was away looking for Rowe Carney, I grew to hate my own people, and to look down on them as being too provincial. He said I only came back here because I'd heard my father was dead and that I was going to inherit, and that once I learned it wasn't so, I was all set to leave again immediately. He said that bringing my ... that bringing you here – his term was even less complimentary than "*gadji*" – was a slap in the face for all Newforest women.

'I tried to counter all his arguments, but there was little I could do. I told them that I loved Newforest and my father, but that I had to leave again soon – and I couldn't tell them why. I had to admit that I loved you and had asked you to marry me, and yet I couldn't tell them anything about you.' He gave a small, mirthless laugh. 'It sounded pretty lame even to me.

'And there they were, nearly two dozen men I've known and respected all my life. Many of them liked me and were trying to help me wriggle out of the mess – but because of the Service's secrecy I couldn't give them any information that would help. They didn't want to condemn me – but I wasn't able to provide them with any strong alternative. The vote, in the end, was unanimous.'

The anger started to grow inside him once more as he continued, 'But that wasn't enough for my damned, self-serving bastard of a brother. There would have been plenty of ways to implement the decision, but Tas insisted that my father pronounce the final decree. My dying father, who was always so proud of me and my accomplishments, who's in constant pain these days ... the others all tried to talk him out of it, but Tas wouldn't let go. My father, no matter how much it pained him, was going to have to be the one to pronounce my sentence, no matter how much it hurt him to do so. I didn't dream Tas could be so cruel as to force him to do that.'

'What ... what is the sentence?' Yvette asked. 'They're

not going to kill you, are they?'

His anger against his brother vented, Pias seemed to lose some of his steam. Walking over to the edge of his bed he sat down and held his head in his hands. 'No, but they might as well have. I've been disowned by my father and my family. They've burned my baby clothes and my wedding shirt, and destroyed all pictures of me. I've been banished from the planet, with all traces of me wiped from their memories. No one of my acquaintance will speak to me, or even acknowledge my presence.'

He lifted his head again and his eyes had a deep, hollow look to them. 'Eve, it's as though I ceased to exist any more.'

CHAPTER SIX

THE CHANTEUSE OF THE IRON ANGEL

Jules left Vonnie to watch over Duke Hanforth and guard their one surviving prisoner while he went out to his car and put a scramble call through to the Head. It took several minutes before Grand Duke Zander von Wilmenhorst could actually get to the vidicom – the hour was late, and he'd been enjoying the small bit of sleep his dual role of Grand Duke and Head of SOTE permitted him. Once on the line, though, he was wide awake and listening with interest as Jules described the events of the evening.

'Get your captive down to our regional office there, pronto,' the Head said when Jules had finished. 'I'll dispatch someone there to handle the interrogation; I know Yvette usually handles that for you, and I want this done as expertly as possible. In the meantime, we've got to put out some sort of cover story to keep the opposition guessing. They'll know by now that their team has run into some trouble. We'll have to keep them from trying again.'

After a brief discussion with Jules, they decided to leak to the press the story that Duke Hanforth of Melenaria had indeed been killed during a premeditated attack on his villa. Although all the attackers had died in the attempt, they had none the less been successful in eliminating their target. Meanwhile, the still-living duke would be kept tightly under wraps – or at least as tightly as anyone could manage to keep *him* – until the day of the wedding. In the meantime, Jules and Vonnie would be pulled off that assignment and instead be given the job of tracking down further the chain of command in the assassination conspiracy.

As he'd been instructed, Jules took his prisoner to the SOTE branch office and stood by while an expert interrogator subtly questioned the killer. Virtually every technique was used short of nitrobarb – and the interrogator assured Jules that this man was not highly enough placed to merit nitrobarb. He was squeezed clean of information even without it.

The information they did get was little enough. This Des-Plainian had served one function only in the organization –

to kill his assigned targets. He had no political convictions, no personal philosophy to uphold, no grudges against Duke Hanforth. He was a total mercenary. His only contact with this organization was through one of the men who had died in the copter crash, a man named Kojomé. Kojomé had been the one to collect all payments and get the orders from the higher-ups. Under even more intensive questioning, this killer did recall Kojomé mentioning a place called the Iron Angel and the name Howard – but whether that was a first name or a last name, he didn't know. No matter how much more they questioned the man, nor how many threats they issued, they could not get any more information out of him than that.

The local SOTE office did have a listing for a nightclub called the Iron Angel, a quite respectable middle-class entertainment spot. There had been no previous suspicion that the club might have any strong links to the underworld, although known bigwigs in local crime organizations had been seen there upon occasion. Nevertheless, this was the only lead they had; Jules and Vonnie would have to follow up on it.

It was mid-morning by the time the interrogation was completed, and Jules put in another call to the Head to discuss strategy and options. Within an hour they had a plan mapped out and they broke connections again; the Head began the backup work to implement the plan while Jules returned to Vonnie and explained what they had learned.

'We're going to have to infiltrate that nightclub,' Jules said. 'The Head and I worked out cover identities for you and me as singer and manager.'

'It shouldn't be hard for me to guess which of us will be which,' Vonnie laughed. 'You couldn't carry a tune if it had chrome-plated handles attached.'

'How's your own voice these days?'

'I haven't done anything formally since leaving the college choir. How does this sound?' She broke into a spontaneous rendition of the Imperial Anthem.

Jules listened and watched her with a dreamy expression on his face. 'That's sweet enough to make me want to spring to attention,' he said. 'You might not be destined to be the recording idol of billions, but it will serve perfectly well for a lounge like the Iron Angel.'

'But I'll need an act, some kind of professional routine ...'

'All being planned. The Head is arranging for Honey Slocum to come up with something for you; from what I'm told, she's one of the best show-business arrangers on Earth. You'll be fantastic, believe me.'

'But how can we be sure the Iron Angel will even hire me?'

'With me as your manager, how could they possibly resist?' Jules grinned.

Two days later, the singer who normally performed at the Iron Angel received an unexpected offer from a talent syndicate on the planet Rumfelt. One of their scouts had spotted her while vacationing on Earth, they said, and he'd been very impressed with her performance. They wanted to sign her to a multi-year exclusive contract involving films, trivision, recordings and personal appearances. The amount of money involved was more than she had ever dreamed of earning – but she would have to leave immediately, because the opening could not be held. Even had she stopped to think about it, she would not have thought there was anything significant to the fact that the planet Rumfelt was located in Sector Four – which was owned by Grand Duke Zander von Wilmenhorst.

Her sudden departure from Earth caught the manager of the Iron Angel – a man named Shorken – completely unprepared. He was angry at her for running out on him without notice, and he was dreading the legions of talent agents who would soon be besieging him with possible replacements. Out of nowhere, though, came a short, chunky man named Willy Bledsoe claiming to have a performer all ready to fill the opening. Bledsoe said he'd heard the spot was vacant from a friend of his on Rumfelt and had been waiting for just such an opportunity. Desperately, Shorken agreed to an audition.

Vonnie – who would now be performing under the name

of Lyla Beaumonde – had been rehearsing constantly for two days under Honey Slocum's able direction. To her pleasant voice had been added a flip, sultry style that was very popular among singers on Earth today, and a few simple dance routines to augment the singing. Vonnie was, fortunately, a quick study; Gospozha Slocum admitted she'd never had a more apt pupil. Thus, by the time Lyla Beaumonde's audition was scheduled, Vonnie was ready to perform.

'I don't think I've been this nervous since being in my grammar-school play,' she admitted to Jules just before going on.

'Relax – and remember, you're not just a singer, you're a *chanteuse* – you've got style. Go out there and knock 'em dead.'

The act was not the most polished show-business performance, but the Iron Angel's manager was not in a position to demand perfection. As he watched and listened to Vonnie, he went over the faked press clippings of her career on the planet Largo that Jules had supplied to him. Everything was in order, and Lyla Beaumonde appeared to have a satisfactory reputation as a steady performer. She would at least satisfy his immediate needs. If she did well at the club, he could keep her on indefinitely; if she didn't, she would at least fill the hole until he could round up some better talent. Before Vonnie had even finished her full act, Shorken called Jules over and they signed a ten-day contract.

If Vonnie had thought she was scared at the audition, the feeling had tripled in intensity by the time of her first show that night. Fortunately it was a Tuesday night, and the audience was only three-quarters of capacity. Still, she had some fidgety moments before she finally overcame both stage-fright and opening-night jitters and settled down to do her act. Her fears were all for naught; the audience loved her, calling her back for two curtain calls. After that she settled down and took to her career with a more professional attitude.

Nine days passed and Lyla Beaumonde began acquiring a good reputation – but that was not exactly what Jules and Vonnie had been aiming for. There were now only two days to go before the Princess's wedding. There had been no assassination attempts against any nobles since the try against Duke Hanforth; perhaps the enemy's forces had been too depleted in that attack and hadn't been rebuilt quickly enough. Or, Jules thought, perhaps they had gained as much as they thought they could and were biding their time until the actual wedding ceremony. Both Jules and the Head were in agreement that *something* was in store for that event, though neither could guess precisely what it was.

And their only lead – this nightclub – was turning cold. There had been no sign of any activity suspicious enough to point the way to a treasonous conspiracy – nothing more criminal than watering the customers' drinks, Jules thought dismally. There had been no sign of anyone named Howard, no sign of Lady A – no sign of any trouble whatsoever. *If I ever want a perfectly safe, boring evening,* Jules thought, *I'll sure know where to come.*

Finally, on Thursday night just before her last show, Gospodin Shorken came to Vonnie's dressing room. 'Make it a good show tonight, Lyla,' he said. 'Abel Howard is in the audience.'

Though her heart jumped, Vonnie managed to keep her face expressionless as she applied her makeup. 'Who's he?' she asked casually.

'Gospodin Howard is one of our big customers – and a very important man. If he likes you, all sorts of good things come your way – provided you play ball with him, if you know what I mean.'

Vonnie knew precisely what he meant, but she knew that it didn't pay to look too smart. 'What do I have to do?' she asked.

'Nothing, just yet. Just go out there and do your act. If Howard likes you, he'll come back here after the show and you can wing it from there.'

As soon as Shorken was gone, Vonnie left her dressing room in search of Jules, who was busy chatting with one of the musicians – and inconspicuously pumping him for any information about shady dealings that might be occurring around the club. Aside from a small amount of illicit drugs and a minor call-girl ring, the man knew nothing. Jules didn't bother with those leads; he was fishing for bigger game.

Vonnie took her fiancé aside and told him of Shorken's visit. 'I was beginning to wonder whether this Howard was a myth,' he said. 'But it all depends on whether we can draw him to our bait.'

'And since when have I ever had trouble attracting a man?' Vonnie asked, rolling her hips suggestively.

'Go a little easier on that,' Jules said, pretending to shade his eyes. 'We only want one man, not the entire audience to come racing up onto the stage after you.' He paced up and down, trying to think of a plan. 'Can you get him to come to your hotel room?' he asked after a bit.

'Do bunnies hop? That's the least of my problems, lover. The more important question is what we're going to do with him once I get him there.'

'Leave all that to me. You just play the dumb, helpless female all the way, no matter what happens. Do whatever he suggests. I'll make sure things don't get out of hand.'

'You'd better,' Vonnie said. 'If I'm going to be unfaithful to you, I'd prefer it to be with someone a little more classy than this Howard character.'

That evening, Vonnie gave the most outstanding performance of her short career. She was called back for six curtain calls, and had projected enough sex appeal to have the men standing in the aisles and whistling. *If all that doesn't hook Howard*, she thought, *I'd better grow a beard and start smoking cigars.*

As she'd hoped, Howard came to her dressing room shortly after she'd finished changing. She took an instant dislike to the big man; she'd seen his kind entirely too many times in the past, and she despised their dehumanizing notions of how to deal with women. But she was playing a role tonight, and she vowed she'd play it to the hilt.

After a remarkably short attempt at small talk, Howard got right to the point. 'I like you, *Lyubovnika*,' he said as though he was handing out the Imperial Medal of Honor. 'How'd you like to go to dinner with me?'

'I've already eaten, and my manager says that I have to watch my weight if I'm going to keep my figure,' she said, all innocent and little-girlish. 'Besides, he's laid down very strict rules for me. He says I'm supposed to go home and go to bed immediately after I finish every night. That way, he says, I won't get all old and wrinkly looking.'

'Sounds like a smooth guy,' Howard cracked. 'Look, did he specify you had to be alone?'

Vonnie giggled coquettishly and shot him a smile that was both ingenuous and knowing at the same time. 'Now that you mention it, I don't believe he did. What did you have in mind, you naughty man?'

Howard told her, in the crudest possible terms. Vonnie didn't have to act to make the blush creep into her cheeks, but her theatrical abilities were taxed to the limit as she forced herself to give him a civil and affirmative answer. Howard smiled, mentally chalking up still another conquest.

They left the club together in his chauffeured car and drove straight to her hotel. She snuggled up to him in the back seat and forced herself to smile as his clammy hands were exploring her body. *The things one does out of loyalty to the Empire!* she thought. *I only hope Jules is quick about whatever plan he has worked out; if this neringo breathes on me too much more, I know I'll throw up.*

They reached the hotel and took the elevator tube up to the eleventh floor where her room was. They walked down the hall together, laughing, and then stood outside her door for a minute as she fumbled through her purse to try to find a key. Finally she located it and opened the door. They stepped inside and she reached for the light switch, but he stopped her. 'We don't need that, do we?' he said. He closed the door behind them, pulled her body tightly against his and began kissing her crudely. At the same time, his hands were behind her, clumsily unfastening her dress.

If Jules doesn't do something soon, Vonnie thought distastefully, *I'll take care of this ape myself. Howard will be walking bowlegged for a week when I get through with him.*

Just then the lights switched on and she heard Jules's voice across the room say, 'Aha! So that's what you've been up to while my back is turned, eh?'

Vonnie backed away from Howard, a look of mock horror on her face. 'Willy, please! You don't understand ...'

'What's there to misunderstand? I've got a picture right here.' He held up a minicamera. 'You in his arms with your dress half off. Thought you could cheat on me, didn't you? Well, I'll fix you. When the newsrolls get their hands on that picture, your career will be finished.'

Howard had been standing aside during this interplay, eyeing the scene scrupulously. He chose this moment to speak. 'I don't think you'll be showing that picture to anyone,' he said calmly.

'No woman cheats on me and gets away with it.'

'Toss it out the airlock,' Howard laughed cruelly. 'I know what your ploy is, and I won't be bummed into it.'

'Ploy?' Vonnie said.

'Sure, I know the old badger game. Want me to tell you how the scene was going to go from there? Lyla here would be pleading with you not to ruin her career, and you'd only laugh at her. Then she'd turn to me and beg me to help. Then I'm supposed to offer to buy the picture from you, and when you think you've taken me for enough money you accept. That's one of the oldest scams around – only I ain't falling for it. You picked on the wrong man, comrades. I'm out of your league altogether.'

Jules, suddenly angry for real – or appearing so – rushed at the bigger man, with murder in his eyes. But it was not the sort of rush that he was capable of; to Vonnie's trained eyes, Jules looked like a slow-motion parody of himself. Howard was able to sidestep him easily and deliver a punch to Jules's right side. Jules fell clumsily, then picked himself up and lunged at the other man again. This time he was able to land a hard blow to Howard's chin that sent the Earthman stumbling backward – but again, Vonnie could tell that he had pulled the punch. Jules could have had Howard unconscious from that blow; instead, the bigger man just shook his head to clear it of the muzziness and came back for more.

The two men locked in combat in the middle of the floor, trading hard punches in rapid succession. Vonnie was tempted to go to her boyfriend's aid, but remembered his instructions that she play the dumb female at all times. She had a glimmering now of Jules's plan, so she meekly backed into a corner and watched, taking care to see that the situation never got too far out of hand.

Both men had bloody lips, and Jules was bleeding from a cut near his eye as well. Each of them appeared to be tiring; the blows were coming less often and the two men were panting heavily. Finally Jules's guard dropped a fraction of a second too long and Howard spotted the opening. He swung a vicious blow into Jules's midsection that doubled the DesPlainian over, and Howard finished him off with a punch that knocked Jules halfway across the room. Jules struggled to get back on his feet, but fell to the ground again, helpless. He lay there, conscious but unmoving.

Howard moved in to finish the job, and Vonnie thought this was a good time to interfere. 'Please, don't kill him!' she exclaimed.

Her voice made Howard stop. He looked back at her, then down at Jules's prostrate form and realized the fight was effectively over. 'You two picked on the wrong man,' he reiterated.

Then a thought crossed his mind. He bent down and lifted Jules up, then tossed him easily across the bed. 'Still, you fought pretty well,' he went on.

'Not well enough,' Jules moaned through lips that were already beginning to swell. 'I lost.'

'Don't take it so personal, there's not many guys can beat me,' Howard boasted. He looked Jules over critically. 'Are you a DesPlainian?'

'Yeah. Been away ten years, though – ran into a little, uh, trouble there.'

Howard nodded. 'Yeah, I know how that is. Listen, I'm a little shorthanded at the moment and I can use a guy who knows how to work with his fists. I still don't like what you tried to do to me, but I figure I paid you back for that. How'd you like to work for me?'

'What do I have to do?'

'Nothing you'll need to grow a conscience for, believe me. All you do is follow orders and get paid pretty well for it.'

'What's "pretty well"?'

'Three hundred a week.'

Jules closed his eyes for a long moment to consider it. Finally he opened them again and looked up at Howard. 'You've got a deal, *tovarishch*.'

Taking a card and a stylus out of his pocket, Howard scribbled an address on the back and then flipped it down beside Jules. 'Be there tomorrow at 9 a.m. sharp, got that?' He started wearily to the door, then turned and looked at Vonnie. 'I'll see you some other time, gossie, when there's fewer interruptions.' And he left the room without further word.

As soon as the door had closed behind him, Vonnie ran to get a damp washcloth to clean up Jules's face. She daubed at the cuts as tenderly as she could, but even so Jules could not help wincing.

'What's the matter, Julie?' she asked as she worked. 'Are you slowing down in your old age?'

'This is no time for impertinence, wench,' Jules said weakly. 'I – ow, that stings! – you don't know how hard I had to work to make sure that dodo disguised as a baboon would win. He was so slow and left me so many openings, I thought *he* was trying to lose, too. I think he wins most of his fights by scalding his opponents to death with hot air.'

He propped himself up on his elbows and grinned. 'But I got what I wanted. I figured that, after the disaster at Duke Hanforth's villa, he'd be in need of some more men. I just had to prove I was crooked enough and a good enough fighter – though not too good. That might have made me seem like a threat. Now that I'm one of his men, we can be in on the inside plans.'

'I still would have liked to take him in for questioning,' Vonnie said. 'There are all sorts of interesting techniques I'd love to use on him.'

Jules shook his head. 'Not just yet. If he were to be picked up two days before the wedding, his group might panic and scatter. We have to capture them all intact, the whole damned organization – and the best way to do that is to let them think everything's fine until we're all set to move. This way may be slower, but it's more certain.'

'I'll phone the Head about this tomorrow before I go over

to meet Howard at this address. Right now I'm going to have to rest a bit. Losing a fight takes a lot out of you – I'll have to try not to make a habit of it. Where are you going?'

'To take a shower,' Vonnie replied. 'Howard had his filthy paws all over me, and I'm going to have to scrub off a whole layer or two of skin before I feel clean again.'

CHAPTER SEVEN

PIRATE ATTACK

Yvette cradled Pias's head against her bosom as he told her of the edict the *kriss* had decreed. She tried to imagine how it would be if her own family turned against her, disowned her, refused even to acknowledge her existence any more. She shuddered. Some things were just too horrible to contemplate. 'Can they actually do that to you?'

'If they choose to ignore me, how can anyone stop them from doing it?'

'They'll have a hard time ignoring you after you become Duke. You'll have troops at your disposal, with the Emperor to back you up if ...'

But Pias was shaking his head. 'You don't understand. I've been *totally* disowned. They no longer recognize me as my father's son. Tas will inherit the title now, not I.'

'That's blatantly illegal,' Yvette cried. 'The Stanley Doctrine guarantees the right of succession by the eldest child, whether he's popular with the local nobility or not.'

'The Stanley Doctrine is fine in theory, but there are plenty of loopholes in practice. Suppose I'd been convicted of murder, for instance. There's plenty of legal precedent to deny me my claim to the title. The *kriss* is a local equivalent of a court, and they've just convicted me of what they consider a pretty heinous crime. Even at best, the issue could be in arbitration for years – and what good would that serve?'

'The Emperor could intervene. I know him personally, and he's a good man. I know he'd see the injustice of all this and decree that you were the lawful duke.'

Pias stood up and walked around the room in a style that reminded Yvette very much of her brother's own pacing while he was considering a problem. '*Khorosho*. Let's suppose for a moment that the Emperor puts his arms around my shoulders and says, "Pias will rule Newforest." Suppose even further that I manage to elude all the assassins Tas then sends against me – that would be his next step, you know. Maybe I can even have him arrested and killed, so that he's no longer a threat.

'What kind of rule would I have? As long as the Emperor kept sending me troops to back up my decisions, I could keep order. But if he ever withdrew them, I'd have to hire a private army from offworld, because no Newforester would follow me, not even the ones who liked me. We're a stubborn people, always have been. So I would rule strictly by force of arms until the day of my death. The people would obey my commands to the minimum degree they could get away with, and not one iota more. I'd have to become a tyrant if I wanted to achieve anything.'

He turned to face her, looking directly into her eyes. 'Eve, I've always felt that a ruler needs the respect and cooperation of his people, and that if he doesn't have that he should step aside for someone who does. I suppose that makes me an archconservative throwback to the days of the democracies on Earth; Bozhe knows they didn't work I've struggled to earn the respect and love of my future subjects...'

'And you've got it,' Yvette interrupted. 'I saw what those people were like today. You're the most popular man on the planet.'

'Maybe up until today. But I know those people, Eve. As soon as word of the *kriss* reaches them they'll fall into line. They've always lived their lives that way and it would take a supernova to budge them. I don't want to force them to be slaves under my rule; I've never been so desperate for power that I'd do anything to keep it. Let my brother have it, if it will make him happy. I have something better for my life – you.'

Yvette blushed and looked down at her feet. 'If it's any consolation,' she said, 'I'm second in line to be Duchess of DesPlaines, right behind my brother Robert.'

'Eve, I wouldn't care if you were a peasant starving in a hovel. You'll always be the Empress of my heart.'

He sat down again beside her and rested a hand on hers. They embraced and kissed for a long, heart-stopping moment, and Yvette felt her love for this gallant and truly noble man renewed a dozenfold. But, once they broke from their embrace again, the ever-practical side of her nature asserted itself.

'What will you do now?' she asked.

Pias stood up and walked to the window. 'Well, it's not as though my life is over,' he said. 'Soon I'll be starting a new career with a new bride. I'm going into exile because of them, so I'm hardly about to throw them away now. You and the Service will be my life; between the two of you, I expect to be too busy to even think of anything else. I'll probably have forgotten all about Newforest after a couple of years.'

But as he gazed out the window at the darkness that covered this hemisphere of the planet he once had been prepared to rule, Yvette could feel the deep sense of loss that was threatening to overwhelm him. Standing, she walked over to him and slipped her arms around his waist.

I'll have to spend the rest of my life making up for the loss I've caused him, she knew. *I only hope it'll be enough*.

Originally, Pias and Yvette had planned to stay on New-forest for six days, and had return reservations on a ship that would take them back to Earth just in time for the Princess's wedding. But this new turn of events left them little reason for staying the additional few days; indeed, an oppressive feeling was building up within them, and the sooner they were off this world the sooner that feeling would go away.

Newforest was an out-of-the-way planet, and was not visited as frequently as most others. Fortunately for Pias and Yvette, however, a chartered passenger ship carrying a group of nobles to Earth for the festivities had developed a minor malfunction nearby, and had stopped on Newforest to have the damage repaired. Yvette learned from calling the spaceport that they would be able to cash in their previous tickets and purchase space on this vessel.

The Bavol manor house seemed almost deserted as they left. Carrying their own bags down the hallways they met not another living soul; the house's occupants were going far out of their way to avoid any contact with them. Pias wanted very much to stop by his father's room and say goodbye, even though he knew the old man would never acknowledge it; but he knew that it would only deepen the pain for both the Duke and himself, and so he forbore doing it.

Outside, a copter was waiting for them, with Yuri to pilot it. The old servant said not a word as he flew them to the spaceport but, as the young couple stepped out, Yuri said, 'Goodbye, Pias.' The two men embraced tearfully and kissed one another; then Yuri got back into the copter and flew away.

Word of the *kriss* had traveled quickly; everyone at the spaceport seemed aware of it. Yvette could see that Pias had been right; whereas yesterday he had been greeted with smiles and enthusiasm, today people turned their heads to avoid seeing him. Yvette had to speak to the ticket clerk; no one would admit that Pias was even there. Pias accepted their behavior stoically, but Yvette could guess just how deeply he was hurt.

Pias stayed in his cabin until the ship, the *Querida*, lifted off the surface of Newforest. Then, with the easing of the heavy gravity, his own cares seemed to ease as well. He emerged from his cabin full of his old gaiety and charm.

'I'm no longer weighted down by responsibilities as the Marquis of Newforest,' he explained to a startled – and delighted – Yvette. 'From now on, I shall be the same carefree, gallant gambler you first met, with a rose in my hatband and a cape around my shoulders. I'll keep the name Pias Bavol, though – I'm damned if I'll let them take *that* away from me, too.'

They quickly introduced themselves to the rest of the passengers on the cruise. Virtually all the others were nobles from the farthest reaches of Sector Twenty-Two, traveling to Earth for the express purpose of seeing the Princess marry her consort. None of them had ever been to Earth before, and the prospect so excited them that they paid little heed to the social distance that ordinarily would have existed between themselves and these two commoners, as they supposed Pias and Yvette to be. All that mattered was that they were going to Earth to see the imperial wedding at Bloodstar Hall.

Pias soon had charmed everyone on board – especially the ladies – with his gallant behavior and entertaining tales.

True to the *persona* he was portraying, he organized an impromptu casino to help while away the time on the long flight back to Earth. In every way, he made himself into the ideal shipboard companion.

The *Querida* made three more scheduled stops for passengers, which lengthened the journey considerably. The ship was nine days out from Newforest when, quite abruptly, alarms began sounding throughout the vessel. Pias was in the gravity-controlled lounge, dealing a hand of five-in-the-hole, when the confusion began. Other people jumped up from the table, sudden panic on their faces. 'What is it?' shrieked one countess. 'Have we hit something?'

'Relax, comrades,' Pias said, pushing his hat back slightly on his head. 'We're in subspace, which is as empty as a drunkard's bottle. There's nothing for us to hit, except maybe another ship – and the odds against that are astronomical. Maybe the captain's just scheduled some sort of drill for us. We have a saying on Newforest: "The wise man worries not about the Devil's shadow." At least wait until we know more about what's happening before you start to panic.'

It was only a few moments later, though, that everyone had real cause for worry. Captain Bacardi's voice suddenly blared over the loudspeaker system, announcing, 'All passengers must return to their quarters immediately and lock themselves in until further notice. Our ship has been approached by a vessel that refuses to identify itself. Until further determination has been made, we must assume that it is a pirate vessel and take appropriate actions. We will be leaving subspace in five minutes. I repeat, all passengers are to lock themselves in their quarters immediately until further notice. Captain out.'

Even Pias's glacial calm could not stop the fear from spreading through the other passengers now. With a mood of hysteria building, the people flocked to the narrow corridors in a desperate attempt to get to their rooms. Nobles who were raised on courtly manners and courtesy were pushing and shoving one another out of the way in their efforts to attain refuge.

Pias managed to locate Yvette in the crush and pulled her

aside out of the main stampede. 'What do you think we should do?' he asked.

'I'm damned if I'll sit in my cabin twiddling my thumbs during a pirate attack,' Yvette said with a tone of even determination. 'This is a small passenger ship, without much of a crew. The captain will need every fighter he can get.'

'He ordered all passengers into their cabins, including us. He'll think we're disobeying orders – and we can't very well go up to him and say, "We're SOTE agents, let us help." '

'So we'll hide until the fighting starts,' Yvette said. 'He's not going to stop in the middle of a battle to reprimand us; and once the battle's over, it won't really matter – one way or the other.'

The two agents took advantage of the confusion to seek out a hiding place. They finally decided on a storage bin where food had been kept, now virtually empty since most of the food had already been eaten during the flight. The crew was in the process of securing the ship from outside attack and proceeding to their battle stations, and they did not notice the pair hiding in the bin. Pias and Yvette settled in to wait for the drop out of subspace, knowing that no action would occur before then.

'Why do you think the pirates would attack this ship?' Pias asked as they waited.

'I don't know. That's been puzzling me, too,' Yvette replied. Most pirates contented themselves with preying on cargo ships; if the cargo was valuable enough, they could sell it for a sizeable profit on the black market. The risk in such cases was minimal; freighters traditionally carried small crews because there was little for them to do while the ship was traveling through subspace. A few of the more daring pirates went after bigger game: the larger luxury spaceliners. The theory was that anyone who could afford to travel on those cruise ships was wealthy; either they would be carrying jewels and other valuables with them, or else they could be held for ransom. For this reason, the liners were usually well armed, and equipped with strong security forces, making an attack upon them a much more dangerous undertaking.

But the *Querida* fit into neither category. It was a compaatively small chartered ship, with no cargo at all and with only thirty-two passengers. While it was true that all the people were important nobles on their own planets, the haul would hardly seem to be worth the pirates' while from an economic point of view. Also, the *Querida* was not running according to a formalized schedule, which should have made it much more difficult for pirates to locate.

Yvette pushed these questions to the back of her mind; she and Pias should deal with the pirates first, and only wonder why afterward.

Standard operating procedure for any vessel under pirate attack was to drop out of subspace immediately and put through a call for help. The subetheric communicator, or subcom, would not work while the ship itself was in subspace; the vessel had to drop back into the regular universe to send out its message and hope that the Imperial Navy would hear and respond in time. There was also the chance that the pirate ship, moving at far greater than light speeds in subspace, would overshoot the now slower-moving target and lose track of it before it could backtrack and pick up the quarry. Finding a spaceship, even a large liner, in the total void of interstellar space made the old needles and haystack problem seem trivial by comparison.

Of course, the pirates also knew that dropping out of subspace was standard procedure. When the *Querida* returned to normal space with a stomach-churning *blump*, the other vessel was right beside it, all set to close and board.

Events began to happen rapidly. The instant they left subspace, the engineer of the *Querida* was on the subcom trying to get through to the nearest naval base. His counterpart on the pirate ship, meanwhile, was activating a special subspace jammer that broke up the normal harmony in the local region of subspace, preventing the message from beaming through. Simultaneously, pirate gunners fired heavy-duty blasters at the stern of their target. The gunners were well-practiced at their task and exceedingly accurate; it took but a single shot to blow out the *Querida*'s engines, leaving the small chartered ship drifting helplessly in space.

With its prey effectively powerless, the pirate ship moved in for the kill. Short bursts from its stabilizing jets pushed it relentlessly toward the *Querida* and, when it was close enough, its hatch opened and a small army of figures clad in battle armor propelled themselves over to the hull of the captured ship. With them, they brought a large box-like contraption called a boarding hatch.

With the efficiency of experts they fitted this boarding hatch over the *Querida*'s normal airlock, then sealed it in place, airtight. That done, they all climbed inside and closed the rear door behind them. They could now force open the airlock of the passenger ship without worrying about damage to the insides; the air would not all rush out in one tornado-like blast, killing people and destroying property.

The leader of the attack squad wielded his hull-torch with authority. In less than five minutes he had cut an opening through the *Querida*'s thick outer plating and was scrambling through with his men at his heels. The crew of the smaller ship had been gathered around the airlock, prepared to welcome the marauders as they deserved, but their lighter-weight blasters were totally inadequate to penetrate the tough battle armor the pirates wore.

The pirates themselves were content to use stunners on their enemies, rendering the *Querida*'s crew senseless for a long enough period to take control of the ship. Then, thinking that most of their organized opposition was disposed of, they ventured deeper into the ship.

When the motors had been destroyed, it also had killed the ultragrav that had been intended for the passengers' comfort. Pias and Yvette, along with the rest of the people aboard the *Querida*, suddenly felt as though the floor had been yanked out from under them. They were in freefall now, but Yvette and Pias knew that sensation well enough to be able to function without handicap.

They emerged from their hiding place and moved toward the airlock, knowing that was where the action would be. As they swam toward it, they could hear the sounds of the short battle, and knew that the crew had been defeated. The *Querida*'s defense would have to be up to them.

Their first step would be to obtain some effective weapons. Both were armed with ministunners that they carried with them, but those would be useless against the battle armor of the pirates. They needed heavy-duty hand blasters – and the only place to get any at the moment was from the pirates themselves.

Hiding once again – this time in the galley – they waited until the procession of pirates passed them, en route to the ship's control room. When the invaders had gone, the two SOTE agents slipped out of their hiding place and swam silently after them. The last pirate in line was lagging a little far behind the rest; Yvette pointed him out as their quarry, and Pias nodded his agreement. As the pirates rounded one corner, Yvette gave the signal to attack.

The two agents launched themselves simultaneously at their intended victim. Pias grabbed the man around the waist, twisting him around and unexpectedly off balance. Meanwhile, Yvette grabbed for the blaster in the pirate's belt holster. Pulling it out hilt first, she slammed the hard surface into the weakest point on the man's armor – his faceplate. The clear glastic shattered, but did not fly to pieces. The man tried to raise his arms to protect his eyes, but Pias had a grip on the arms now and would not let them go. Yvette made another strike with her impromptu hammer, and this time the glastic broke apart, cutting the man's face to ribbons. Yvette followed up by sending her fist through the opening in the suit. Her punch connected solidly with the pirate's nose, knocking his head back against the hard interior surface of his helmet. His body instantly went limp as he lapsed into unconsciousness.

Unfortunately, all the suits of space armor had been com-linked by radio. At the first sensation of Pias hitting his suit, the hapless pirate had yelled out a startled exclamation. It was nothing coherent, but it served to notify his fellows that all was not well behind them. Curious, they turned to see what was happening.

By this time, Yvette had her blaster turned around in her hand and ready to fire. A deadly bolt of energy leaped from the barrel of her gun toward the armored figures at the end of the corridor. Her aim was true; the beam hit one man squarely in the chest, burning through the heavy metal of his armor and searing the skin underneath. Through the hole that was now in his suit, she could hear his scream of agony echoing down the hallway.

Pias, meanwhile, was unarmed – but not helpless. Using

as a missile the now-limp body of the pirate they'd attacked, he hurled it the length of the corridor, scattering the pirates at the other end. Then, fearlessly, both he and Yvette leaped forward to press their attack.

Had they been working under even some slight gravity conditions, they might have had a chance. The battle armor was heavy, slowing down the pirates' reactions; Pias and Yvette, both from heavy-grav worlds and unencumbered, could move like lightning in comparison. But in order to make the most efficent use of their speed, they needed some constant surface to work on, a continual direction to move toward. That was lacking in freefall. The agents had only one gun between them, while all their opponents were armed and armored.

The buzzing of stun-guns filled the air as the pirates tried to counter this unexpected attack. Despite their quickness, Pias and Yvette could not dodge all the beams at once and, within seconds, they were floating unconscious in the middle of the corridor.

It was several hours later when they finally regained consciousness. Things were fuzzy for another ten minutes as the effects of the stun wore off slowly; sounds seemed to increase and decrease like a siren, while objects would snap into visual focus for a second and then frustratingly retreat into oblivion once more.

They were still in space; they could tell that instantly from the lack of gravity. Their bodies were drifting in an open, lighted room. Looking around, they could see other people floating about them; as things came more and more into focus, they could tell that the room was the *Querida*'s lounge and the other people were their fellow passengers and the crew of the ship. A pair of pirates guarded the door, stun-guns at the ready. Their quick, darting eyes indicated they were keeping vigilance; there would be no way to get the drop on them with a surprise rush.

Pias's head hurt. He had never been stunned before and, although it was preferable to stopping a blaster beam, he could not favorably recommend the experience. *It may be a non-lethal way to stop people*, he thought, *but it's still far from kind*.

When the others saw them stirring they came over and asked if everything was all smooth. Yvette assured them that, aside from the after effects of the stun, they were in good shape, but a little confused about what was happening. One earl filled them in.

After the abortive battle, the pirates had herded everyone into this one lounge area so they could all be kept under surveillance in one place. Then the ship had been rigged up in tandem with the pirate vessel so that the larger ship could tow the *Querida* to its base. So far, the pirates had made no attempt to hurt anyone, for which the passengers were most grateful. They knew, however, that such a state of affairs could not continue forever.

They must be doing this for the ransom, then, Yvette thought – and yet, some part of her mind was telling her that was not the case at all. But no explanation for this behavior occurred to her, so she dropped the speculation and did her best to maintain order among the captives.

Pias found his hat floating in the air some distance away; the pirates had been considerate enough to toss it in here after him. Retrieving it, he checked the holster hidden behind the rose on the brim; the ministunner he kept for emergencies was still there. Feeling a little better, he donned the hat once more and, like Yvette, bided his time until the situation altered.

Four hours later their trip ended. Everyone was herded out of the lounge, down the corridors and out the airlock through a pressurized tube. There were faint sensations of gravity, just slightly more than none at all; Yvette surmised that the pirates' headquarters was on some asteroid, a piece of junk floating in the empty spaces between the stars. Interstellar debris like that made ideal locations for secret bases, because they were almost impossible to find unless one knew the coordinates in advance.

The captives were marched down a ramp and into a small room where they were crowded together. A man of Oriental ancestry in a well-tailored, heavily braided uniform sat at a table before them, with three men standing at attention behind him. He would ask each person for his identity, and check it against a printed list he had; then each passenger would be taken out of the room through a side entrance.

The line moved quickly, and after only three minutes it was the SOTE agents' turn. They stepped forward together as the pirate chief motioned to them. 'Your names?' he asked abruptly.

'Pias Bavol, and this is my fiancée, Yvette Dupres.'

The man searched his list through twice for those names and couldn't find them. 'You're lying,' he said at last. 'There are no such people listed on the original manifest.'

'We weren't scheduled to be on board,' Yvette said. 'We got on at Newforest, when the ship made an unscheduled stop for repairs.'

The man stared at them for several seconds as he chewed on the end of his stylus. 'That would make sense,' he mused, mostly to himself. 'It would also explain why the ship was so late getting here.'

Yvette's mind was racing as she assimilated all the data coming in. These pirates had had advance warning of everyone who was supposed to be on the ship and of its exact flight plan. While pirates usually tried to learn some details of a flight before deciding whether to attack it, knowledge in this depth presupposed an intelligence network far broader than that possessed by the average space buccaneer. Yvette scanned her inquisitor a little more closely.

As she stared, her eyes picked up a detail they had missed in her first casual glance – a detail almost unnoticeably tiny. Around this man's neck was a silver chain, from which dangled a single integrated circuit chip. Yvette had seen necklaces like that before; they were worn as identification symbols by the top minions of Lady A's conspiracy. If this pirate was a part of that organization, it would indeed explain why his advance information was so thorough. It also meant that this raid was likely to be of far more significance to the Empire than merely holding some nobles hostage.

The pirate chief was looking at Pias with a quizzical expression on his face. 'Bavol of Newforest?' he asked. 'Are you by chance any relation ...?'

'No,' Pias said. 'None whatsoever.'

The man shrugged and made a small notation on his list. Then, turning to one of his henchmen, he said, 'These two are of no importance to us whatsoever. Take them away and dispose of them at once.'

CHAPTER EIGHT

TRAPPED

The morning after the fight in the hotel room, Jules reported to the address he'd been given by Howard. The building turned out to be a gymnasium in a less respectable part of the city. Its fake bricks were weathered, its façade grimy, the lettering on its sign barely readable. It was a hangout for punks on their way up, athletes on their way down, and a good many nonentities who were going nowhere at all and were in no rush to get there.

As Jules walked in, the smell of stale sweat filled his nostrils. There were the repeated thumping sounds of fists hitting punching bags and the moans of men in less than perfect condition overtaxing their muscles in an effort to look in shape. Jules thought briefly on how little change there had actually been in gymnasia since the days of the ancient Greeks. The equipment the men used for their training grew ever more sophisticated with the passing years, but the basic activities remained the same — because the human body remained the same.

Jules looked the place over quickly, then walked over to the man at the equipment window. 'A man named Howard told me to report here this morning,' he said, showing the card he'd been given.

The equipment manager took the card and stared at it as though it were something entirely new in his life. Jules could see his lips move as he read it, could almost see the thought processes seeping slowly through the man's dim brain. 'Yeah,' the fellow said at last. 'Meeting's upstairs, room D-5.' He handed the card back to Jules.

Jules found the stairs and went up to the indicated room. Inside he found about a dozen other men seated in chairs that were arranged in rows, classroom style. There was no sign of Howard, so Jules took a seat to wait. None of the other men paid him much attention after their initial once-over.

More men arrived and took their seats, until the room was filled. Five minutes later, Abel Howard entered. He was dressed casually, but there was a tough look about his face that told Jules this man was anything but casual.

'Let's get one thing straight first off,' Howard began. 'If any of you think working for me is going to be easy, you can leave now. You're all here because the people I had before are dead. There's a chance you'll end up that way yourself. If that scares you, you don't belong here.'

No one made a move towards the door, but a few did shift around nervously in their seats. 'What the hell,' one man at the back commented. 'We're all going to die sometime, right? Why not get paid for it?'

His joke drew a nervous laugh from the other men.

Howard waited for the laughter to subside, then continued. 'The second thing I want to get across here is that I'm the boss. You're getting paid to do what I tell you – not to think, not to ask the guy next to you what he thinks, but to do what I say. I don't have to pay someone to argue with me or question my judgment. If anyone thinks that'll be too much of a strain on him, get out.'

Again, no one moved.

'I'm glad we understand each other. Our first job is going to be tomorrow afternoon. It'll be rough. You all report here at ten in the morning and I'll supply you with everything you need.'

'Just what will we be doing?' one man asked when it became obvious that Howard was not about to elucidate.

'What did I just say about asking questions?' Howard barked. 'What does it matter what you'll be doing? You'll do what I tell you, that's all.'

'I think he meant,' Jules spoke up, 'that it might be easier for us to prepare ourselves for the job if we had a rough idea of what we were supposed to do. There's a difference in preparation for babysitting and for bank robbing.'

Howard gave him a black look. 'You'll know when I know,' he growled, 'Don't worry, you'll get all the preparation you need.'

Howard's reaction told Jules a great deal. It was clear that the boss didn't know either what was going to be done – and his testiness was an indication that he himself was not happy with that state of affairs. Abel Howard was a man who liked holding the upper hand; being someone else's underling was an irksome experience for him. It would take a powerful person to hold him in a subordinate position – and Jules had a good idea who that person must be.

The fact that the operation would be tomorrow afternoon was critical – that was when Crown Princess Edna would be married in a state ceremony of enormous proportions. The coincidence was too great to expect Howard to have some other target in mind, considering that he'd already been involved in attempts to kill members of the nobility. Howard was an element in a treasonous plot, of that Jules now had no doubts at all. And to his mind, that suggested Lady A.

He had seen Lady A in action only once, on the tape he and Yvette had captured during their adventure on Sanctuary. That little bit, though, had convinced him that the lady was no one to take lightly. She would be perfectly capable of putting Howard in his place; and Howard would particularly bridle at having to take orders from a woman.

Howard made a few more general comments and had everyone leave a number with him where they could be reached if he needed them. Then he dismissed them, reminding them to meet back here at ten tomorrow morning.

Jules returned to his hotel room and spent half an hour taking the vidicom set apart. With the unit's innards spread all over his bed, he took a small device from a drawer and attached it to two other leads, then reassembled the set. Although it had been a tiny change, it was a very important one; this vidicom now had a SOTE scrambler unit, and was secure for classified calls.

With that accomplished, he put in a call to the Head back in Florida. He explained in detail what he and Vonnie had learned so far, and he gave his own personal suspicions about Lady A's involvement. As always, the Head listened with rapt attention as Jules spoke – and as always, his agile mind was computing, planning, re-evaluating everything on the basis of what he heard.

When Jules finished his report, the Head leaned back in his chair. 'The alternatives as I see them are as follows,' he said. 'First, we could have this Howard picked up immediately. That would be a very short-sighted action, since it would alert his superiors that we're onto them and they could escape untouched. I discarded that plan instantly.

'Second, I could put out a full surveillance on him, cover him with so many agents and bugs that he won't even be able to go to the 'fresher in privacy. We could check out everyone he sees between now and the wedding, trace all his calls – if he hasn't gotten his orders yet, he has to get them sometime in the next twenty-four hours. I'd like us to know them just as soon as he does.

'But, if Lady A is involved in this – and my hunch, like yours, says there's a high probability of that – I can't help but be haunted by what she said on that tape, that her organization is aware of nearly everything we do. I've made no headway thus far in plugging the leak; everyone on the staff checks out loyal to twelve decimal places, and every square millimeter of every office has been examined thoroughly for bugs. There's simply no way she can know what she obviously knows, and it's driving me crazy.

'At any rate, *if* her boast is true, putting a blanket around Howard would be as bad as pulling him in directly. It would tip our hand that we know something is about to happen, at which point Lady A would simply ditch him and switch to another tactic that we might not discover in time. For obvious reasons, we prefer the devil we know to the devil we don't.'

SOTE's top officer tilted his head slightly to the side and looked at Jules. 'That leaves me with alternative number three. That is, to leave you and Vonnie right where you are and let you continue your own surveillance until the last possible moment. Hopefully the conspiracy will commit itself to a plan of action and won't be able to back out in time to prevent us from closing our net. We – and you – would be walking a tightrope, and one slip could mean disaster.'

'I've walked plenty of tightropes in my life, and I've managed them all so far,' Jules smiled.

His boss returned the expression. 'Remind me never to use circus metaphors around you; they can be interpreted too literally. But I hope I made my meaning clear. We would have to wait long enough to make sure Lady A and her group have committed their forces to their plan beyond recall; but if we wait too long, we might not be able to take effective enough action against it. With the welfare of the Empire at stake, waiting is an awfully dangerous game.'

Jules's smile disappeared and he was as deadly serious as his superior. 'I certainly understand that, sir. But let's face it – until we can plug that leak, it's the only game we can play.'

The Head nodded. 'I just wanted to make sure you understood the situation fully before agreeing to it.'

'I do. In fact, I already came to the same conclusions myself. That's where Vonnie is right now, keeping an eye on Howard. She'll report in the instant anything happens.'

The Head sighed. 'You certainly know how to make an old man feel unnecessary. But then, that's why you're my best agent. Keep me posted on everything – and good luck, Jules.'

'Thank you, sir.' But even as Jules spoke, his boss's image was fading from the screen.

Yvonne Roumenier was highly skilled at the delicate art of trailing a suspect. She had accompanied Jules to the gym for the meeting, waiting outside in his car. Jules took a cab back to the hotel when he left, leaving Vonnie with the supervehicle for her own use.

The female agent waited around outside the gym for another two hours before Howard emerged from the building once again, got into his groundcar and drove off. Vonnie had surreptitiously slipped a beeper under the body of his vehicle, so she had no difficulty following him across town without being conspicuous. Howard gave no indication that he suspected he was being tailed. He went directly to a restaurant, the Chez Gaston, and went inside. Vonnie followed him in.

When her eyes became accustomed to the darker interior, she looked around and saw her quarry seated at a table with a very beautiful woman. The two talked for half an hour – the woman calmly, the man with a variety of gestures and emphasis. At the end of their meal, the woman handed Howard a thick brown envelope, got up from the table and left the restaurant. Vonnie hesitated; should she follow this contact, find out who she was and what she was doing, or should she stay with Howard and check him out further? She decided on the latter course. Howard *was*, after all, her assignment; she was curious about the contents of that envelope. And besides, she had gotten enough pictures of the woman on her minicamera; hopefully SOTE would be able to run an ident check from those.

Had Vonnie known who she was observing, she might have decided differently. But, like all but five people in the Service of the Empire, she had never heard of Lady A, and she did not realize the importance of that one person in the plot against the Empire. She had no way of knowing that, no matter how many photos she took of the woman, the Service would never be able to correlate them with Lady A's identity, because Lady A did not officially exist in any of its files. The course of galactic history might have been significantly altered had Vonnie chosen to follow the woman; but, through no fault of her own, she did not do so. Given what she knew at the time, her decision was the correct one.

Howard finished his meal alone, paid the bill and left. Vonnie was right after him, though she took great care to make sure he didn't spot her. Howard drove out of the city proper, into the hills; Vonnie stayed a respectable distance away so that he wouldn't realize anyone was following him. This was an expensive neighbourhood, but Vonnie doubted Howard had too many financial worries. Her quarry stopped his car in the driveway of a large house, got out, unlocked the door and went inside.

Vonnie parked a short distance further up the hill and waited. This was probably Howard's home, and there was no telling how long he might stay here. Vonnie chafed. She wanted to break in there to get a look at whatever had been in the envelope the woman in the restaurant had handed Howard, and she wanted to be able to put a tap on his vidicom line – but she could do neither while he was there. All she could do was wait until he had left before making her break-in.

In the meantime, she called Jules back at the hotel. Her fiancé had by this time completed his own call to the Head and was waiting eagerly for her report. She gave him the location of Howard's house and then a brief rundown on Howard's activities so far.

Jules's interest picked up enormously when Vonnie mentioned the woman Howard had met for lunch. 'What did she look like?' he asked, trying his best to make his voice sound casual.

'Dark hair, light complexion, medium height, extremely beautiful but very cold. I think she'd give an iceberg goose bumps. It would be hard to guess her age; I'd say maybe forty, but *very* well kept up. She dressed stylishly. Sound like anyone you know?'

Jules was cursing the luck that had let Vonnie spot her rather than himself. 'I'm not sure,' he lied. 'It might be a good idea, though, to investigate her a bit if you happen to run across her again. We have to check all leads.'

'*Khorosho*, will do. In the meantime I'll just have to wait here for Howard to leave again so I can investigate inside. *A bientôt.*

It was more than an hour before Howard emerged once again from his house and drove off down the hill. Vonnie waited another five minutes to be sure he hadn't forgotten anything and come right back, and then she slipped out of her own car and walked around to the back of Howard's house.

The windows were all closed, and Vonnie could tell from the special sensors she carried in her utility belt that there was a burglar-trapping system. If any unauthorized person touched the window while the system was in operation, it would ring alarms and give the intruder a severe electrical shock – not enough to kill, perhaps, but certainly sufficient to knock an adult unconscious until help could arrive. It was a sophisticated device, and it took Vonnie a full ten minutes to circumvent it with the tools she'd brought with her. That task accomplished, she forced the window open and entered the house.

She found herself in a small pantry just off the kitchen. Walking quietly through the house she came to the living room, but a quick look around told her there was nothing of interest for her here. Continuing, she came to the study. On the desk was the envelope she had seen Howard take at the restaurant, and in the ashtray beside it were the remains of whatever message it had contained. Vonnie sighed slightly. She wished she'd been able to get to it before Howard had burned it, but she was not a person to dwell on might-have-beens. Taking a small, empty cylinder from her belt, she emptied the ashes of the note into it. The lab technicians at SOTE headquatrers were experts at reconstructing evidence from the most trivial seeming of scraps; perhaps they could make something out of these ashes. It would at least be worth a try.

Howard's home vidicom was a wall unit, one of the large, ostentatious models that took up an entire side of the study with its screen. She grimaced again. Taking one of those apart to plant a tap on the line would not be an easy task; she only hoped Howard would stay away a bit longer while she worked on it.

She set to the job with grim determination, and soon had dismantled the appropriate parts of the vidicom. Taking a handful of electronic components from the pouch at her waist, she began connecting them into the circuit. She had a more difficult time of it than Jules had had attaching the scrambler to his hotel set, because this tap was more complicated. It was capable not only of intercepting the messages that went in and out over this line and broadcasting them to a special receiver Vonnie had in her car, but also of tracing back any incoming calls so that Vonnie and Jules would know where any message was originating.

So intent was Vonnie about her business that she almost didn't hear the noise until it was too late. There was the slight swishing sound of loose clothing, the soft padding of bare feet along the carpet. Startled, Vonnie looked up and found herself staring into the muzzle of a stun-gun.

The person holding the gun was a young woman, no more than twenty by Vonnie's estimation and ravishingly beautiful. She was wearing nothing but a loose-fitting silken bathrobe that reached only halfway down her thighs. *A live-in girlfriend*, Vonnie thought. *Damn! I should have suspected there might be someone else around. But everything was so quiet!*

The girl must have been sleeping toward the back of the house, and been awakened by some slight noise Vonnie made. Thinking there was a burglar, she put on the robe and took the gun Howard kept for protection, walking down the hallways barefoot in her attempt to sneak up on the intruder. The poor girl was both very brave and very frightened; she clutched the stun-gun tightly with both hands, and even so the weapon was shaking as she pointed it at Vonnie.

Had the SOTE agent been an ordinary burglar, the stunner might have proved an effective deterrent; but Vonnie, as both a DesPlainian and a highly trained espionage agent, was not about to let so simple a thing stop her, particularly when it was being wielded by such an obviously inexperienced woman.

Even as the stun-gun buzzed, Vonnie was in motion. Her movements were so quick that they looked like a mere blur to the startled Earthwoman. One moment her target had been kneeling on the floor, and the next moment the interloper was coming quickly toward her. Her first shot landed harmlessly on the carpet where the woman had been; she had no time for a second. Vonnie gave her a gentle tap on the side of the neck – gentle, that is, for a DesPlainian – and Howard's girlfriend sank to the floor, unconscious.

Vonnie debated what to do now. If she left the girl behind, she'd call the police as soon as she woke up and tell them she'd interrupted a burglar working on the vidicom set. It would take only a minor inspection to discover the tap, and Howard would know his plans were compromised. That could not be allowed to happen.

On the other hand, Vonnie respected innocent human life too much to kill the girl simply because she'd been in the wrong place at the wrong time. To the best of Vonnie's knowledge, Howard's girlfriend was guilty of no more than bad taste in men, and did not deserve to die simply for trying to stop a burglar breaking into her man's house.

In the end, Vonnie decided to take the girl with her. She could be dropped at the local SOTE office and held incommunicado for two days, until this whole affair was over. Howard would wonder where she had disappeared to; he might even be concerned enough to call the police and report her disappearance, though Vonnie doubted it. But in no case would he be able to make the connection between his girlfriend's vanishing and possible surveillance and monitoring activities directed against him.

This unexpected interruption did make Vonnie feel nervous, though. She finished her job with a rush, not wanting to come across any further surprises, then looked around to see where the study window was. She didn't want to carry the girl's body all the way back to the pantry window she'd originally used and, in her nervousness, carelessly overlooked the obvious solution of going out of the front door.

She realized her mistake the instant she touched the window. Each of the windows in this house had been rigged with the burglar deterrent system independently of the others; her shorting out one had not affected the rest of them. It was not at all a common arrangement, but it was one she knew she should have checked for none the less; she cursed herself for her sloppiness.

But her thoughts came far too late. Even as the idea formed in her mind, a strong electrical shock surged through her body. With a loud, involuntary groan, she pulled away from the window sill and fell to the floor, unconscious.

It did not take Howard very long to figure out the truth. When he returned home his girlfriend Charla was just starting to recover consciousness, while Vonnie was still out completely. When Charla told him what 'Lyla Beaumonde' had been doing, Howard's mind leaped to the inevitable conclusion.

She and Bledsoe must be working together on this, he thought. *I'll have to do something to make sure they're stopped*.

He considered telling Lady A and asking her opinion, but decided against it. She would be paying him good money for the job tomorrow, and if he told her he'd been shadowed she might decide to cancel her plans – which would leave him in a bad financial situation. He had already contracted with his own men, and he'd have to pay them or risk their anger. Besides, she already thought of him as inferior; he didn't want to confirm that opinion by seeming to have slipped so easily into this net. As long as he took care of these two spies himself, everything should be smooth.

He made two calls – the first to one of his more trust-worthy men, and the second to Jules. 'Bledsoe, I've got another quick little job for you.'

'Oh?' Jules asked. 'What is it?'

'What do you care? Just get over to my house right away.' He gave the address, adding, 'If you're not here in an hour, you can forget about tomorrow.'

Jules was suspicious of this sudden move – it didn't seem to fit into the pattern. In addition, he hadn't heard from Vonnie in a couple of hours, and he was becoming worried. But there was little he could do; he had to stay on Howard's good side until he learned what the plans were for tomor-row. He took a cab up to Howard's home and knocked on the front door.

'Come in,' Howard said – and the instant Jules complied, he was shot down with a stunner beam set on four – a two-hour stun. He fell to the ground without even having time to wonder how his identity had been discovered.

'Take him and the girl out in your car,' Howard told his henchman. 'See to it that they have an accident – but somewhere far away from here, understand?'

The other man nodded. He was very good at arranging accidents.

CHAPTER NINE

THE GRATE ESCAPE

Yvette and Pias were both startled at the abruptness of the death sentence pronounced over them by the pirate leader. Whatever the plot was in which he was involved, it obviously was concerned only with those passengers who were of noble birth ... and while both SOTE agents actually were, they had denied it as part of their cover identities. For that, they were to die.

One guard stepped forward from against the wall behind his leader. 'The usual method?' he asked.

The boss nodded. 'Yeah. Space 'em.'

Both agents shuddered at the thought. Being tossed out an airlock without a spacesuit and exposed to the deadly vacuum was not a pleasant way to die. Though neither had ever witnessed such a death personally, they were well aware of the consequences of exposure to such a hostile environment. Even if the victim tried to hold his breath for a while, other effects entered the picture. Without external air pressure on the skin, the body bloated and blew up like a balloon. The blood literally began boiling in his veins, rupturing small capillaries and sending the fluid bubbling out of mouth, nose, ears and other orifices. The thin layer of protective liquid over the eyes evaporated, leaving them dry and unprotected; unless the lids were kept tightly shut the eyes could even pop like two grapes under pressure. Eardrums ruptured as a matter of course. At this point, even the most stoic of heroes would have to cry out in pain, expending the last little bit of air in his lungs and causing them to collapse...

Small wonder that spacing was one of the most feared punishments in human society. *Give me a nice, clean blaster bolt through the brain, any day*, Yvette thought.

The guard stepped around behind the two SOTE agents and pushed them forward; they practically flew across the room in the low gravity. 'Get moving!' the pirate told them. 'You heard what Ling said – we ain't got all day.'

Yvette and Pias allowed themselves to be herded out the front door into a narrow, dimly lit corridor beyond.

'Straight ahead,' their guard insisted, motioning with his stunner to emphasize the point. 'Turn right at the end, through the door to the Air Recycling Plant.'

The agents did as they were told, making their march as long and drawn out as they could. A dozen plans occurred to them within those seconds, and were discarded as impractical just as quickly. They both knew Pias had his ministunner hidden behind the large red rose on the brim of his hat. They had to make sure he would get the chance to use it ... and that they would have a chance to escape afterward. This corridor was a little too crowded, with too great a risk of their break being discovered immediately. They waited, hoping that the next few minutes would provide them with a better opportunity.

When they reached the end of the hall, they turned through the designated doorway as ordered. The Air Recycling Plant for the pirate base was immense. A giant plastic dome arched over their heads. If the asteroid on which the base was located had been circling a star the dome would have been transparent to let in the light and heat; but since this asteroid was at least a lightyear from any star, the dome was opaque and covered with series of bright spotlights shining down upon rows and rows of growing green plants that stretched for more than a hundred meters into the distance. The photosynthesis of these plants could not provide all the oxygen a base of this size required, of course; further along, Pias and Yvette could see a large rock-crusher. Robots would be sent out to mine the asteroid itself for oxygen-bearing minerals, which would then be brought back to the base and broken down into their components. Such an operation was standard for any base, legal or not, on an airless world; it had long since been discovered that planetoids of any reasonable size contained enough trapped oxygen to supply a human base with its needs indefinitely.

With the exception of themselves and their guard the plant seemed entirely deserted. This was what they had been hoping for. Tending a plant like this was hard, dirty work, and so the pirates had made sure it was completely automated. After all, one reason they were pirates was to avoid honest labor if at all possible.

Pias took off his hat and wiped his forehead with his sleeve. 'Hot in here, isn't it?' he said. 'I guess all those lights in this enclosed space build up a greenhouse effect.' He put his hat back on his head – but during that maneuver, he had been able to take his ministunner from its hidden holster and palm it in his hand.

'Yeah, something like that,' the pirate said. He had not been chosen for either his scientific knowledge or his loquacity. 'You won't have to worry about it much longer.'

'Ah yes, the very subject I was going to bring up next. While Yvette and I are not nobles, and therefore of no interest to your boss, we both are quite rich – and that might be of possible value to you. If you were to help us get out of here, we could make it well worth your while.'

'I'll help you get out of here,' the pirate grinned sadistically. 'Right through that airlock over there.'

'No, you misunderstand me,' Pias said, injecting the proper note of desperation into his voice. 'If you were to steal a ship and take us to the nearest planet where there's a bank, I think we could reward you well. How does fifty thousand rubles sound?'

'It sounds crazy, *tovarishch*. If I set one foot on a planet with you, I'd be arrested immediately. Why should I betray my comrades to save your drapping necks?'

They had reached one side of the dome, and were now standing beside an auxiliary airlock. The guard gave them another evil grin. 'Get inside, both of you.'

There was no more time; they would have to act now. But the guard had his blaster already drawn and pointed at them. His attention would have to be distracted for the split second it would take Pias to aim and fire his own gun, or their only chance might be gone for good. Realizing this, Yvette took a step away from Pias.

'Maybe there are some things *I* can offer you that your comrades can't,' she said in a sultry voice. She began unbuttoning the top buttons of her blouse. 'It must get awfully lonely here on this base. Wouldn't you like someone to help you keep away the cold on the long, empty nights?'

Her voice was filled with a thousand promises, and the view being offered was a glimpse of paradise itself. No healthy heterosexual male could have resisted the opportunity to take an extra long glance in Yvette's direction, even if he had no serious thoughts about taking her up on her offer. The pirate guard fell prey to the trap, and it proved his undoing.

Pias took the chance when it was offered. As the pirate diverted his gaze to Yvette, the Newforester brought up his small weapon and fired. The pirate dropped to the ground, the last thought in his mind being the sight of Yvette's plunging *décolletage*.

'What took you so long?' Yvette asked as she buttoned up her blouse again. 'I nearly had the whole thing off before you shot him.'

'I'm a man too, my love,' Pias replied. 'Aren't I entitled to look? If I'm going to marry you, I should have the right to inspect the merchandise once in a while.' He walked over and nudged the limp body with his foot. 'What'll we do with him? He'll only be out for two hours.'

'We'll need a longer head start than that. If he doesn't report back to his boss he might not be missed for a long time; but if we just leave him bound and gagged somewhere, someone might discover him prematurely.' She paused. 'Much as I hate to do it to anyone, I think *that* may be our only answer.' And she gestured with her head to indicate the airlock.

Pias nodded grimly. 'I'm still pretty new to killing, but I'm afraid I have to agree. He was, after all, more than willing to do it to us. At least he'll have the benefit of being unconscious when it happens – and maybe his ghost will get satisfaction from knowing he'll haunt my conscience every once in a while.'

He bent down to help Yvette drag the body across the floor and into the airlock, even though he knew his fiancée was quite strong enough to do it herself. 'At least the last thing he saw in his life was a sight of incredible beauty,' Pias said, but Yvette ignored the flattery.

They closed and dogged the inner door, then Pias turned the knob that would open the outer one. Neither of them looked through the small window at what was happening to the body of the pirate who'd been about to kill them. Instead, they walked a few meters away from the door before saying another word.

'I suppose our next move,' Pias said, his voice barely more than a whisper, 'is to steal a ship and get out of here. Once we're back on an inhabited planet, we can report what's happened.'

'Can you fly a ship?' Yvette asked.

'Never had the time to learn.'

'Same here. Jules always handled that department. I specialized in other things.'

'We could always ask Ling and his men if they'd be so kind as to fly us home.'

'Cynicism ill becomes you, *mon cher*. Things aren't that hopeless yet. With luck, we'll have between two and six hours before our escape is detected. That should be time to do a great number of things. Let's scout out the territory before we make any hasty plans.'

They inspected the rest of the Air Recycling Plant with a closer eye for detail. The dome was big and empty except for the greenery and its maintenance equipment, plus the mining and oxygen separation machinery. 'No one seems to come here very often,' Pias observed. 'It might be a good place to hide out.'

'If they really get a search party organized, this is one of the first places they'd look,' Yvette pointed out. 'We couldn't hide from a systematic search, not in here.'

Pias shook his head and looked at his feet. 'Sometimes, darling, you make me feel very stupid and incompetent at this business.'

She ran a hand through his curly brown hair. 'Cheer up. You've only been at this a couple of months. I grew up on it, remember? Don't worry, you'll learn.'

Against one wall of the dome they found the pumps that forced the rejuvenated air down into the labyrinth of underground tunnels that made up the base. 'Oh, what I wouldn't do for a few liters of tirascaline right now,' Yvette said. 'Pouring that into the system would put everybody to sleep in minutes and we could go around tying them up at our leisure.'

Pias was spending more of his time eyeing the ducts themselves. 'These are enormous,' he commented. 'I guess they have to be, for workmen to get inside and repair them if anything goes wrong.'

He and Yvette looked at one another simultaneously, smiles lighting up both their faces. 'And they go all around the base,' Yvette continued his thought. 'They could take us anywhere we want to go. You see, *mon amour*, I have no monopoly on brilliant ideas.'

Pias grimaced. 'But the same problem applies. Once they know we're on the loose, they'll start looking, and the idea may occur to them, too. It wouldn't be too difficult to flush us out of the ventilating system if they really wanted to.'

Yvette pondered that for a long moment, wondering what her brother would do under the circumstances. While she knew that she was, by a very slight margin, the more insightful of the pair, Jules was usually the one who came up with the better plans. *I've gotten too used to letting him do certain things*, she thought. *I should develop my own talents independently.*

'There's got to be a way around that,' she said at last. 'Let's give it a little chance to formulate in our minds. In the meantime, we're very exposed right now if any pirate should happen by here. Let's get into the ventilating ducts now and worry about escape while we're out of sight. How do we get this grating off?'

Pias studied the way the grate was fastened in place. 'There looks to be some hooks holding it from the inside.' He reached his hand through the slot and extended his arm through as far as he could. After a couple of tries, the latch unhooked and Pias was able to pull one side of the grill away from the opening. After unhooking the latch on the other side, the entire grating came away and they were able to get inside the duct itself.

Because of their comparatively short height as natives of high-grav planets, they discovered that they were able to stand up straight within the duct. The interior of the tunnel was dark and the floor was quite smooth, making walking hazardous, but there were handholds placed at intervals in the walls for the convenience of workmen who might someday need to make interior repairs.

'This is a great system,' Pias said as he pulled the grate back into place behind them. 'We can travel anywhere we want throughout the base, open the grill from the inside and leave, then come back in when we want without anyone knowing it, if we're careful not to be seen. Let's go exploring, shall we?'

They began walking carefully and quietly through the large metal tunnel. The floor sloped downward toward the planetoid's interior, indicating that most of the base was located beneath the ground level. Yvette had been expecting that; it was much easier to dig tunnels into the rock to make an underground village than to build a dome over a surface one. The native rock would insulate against the worst extremes of temperature, and all it would require was a little airproofing to make sure the atmosphere didn't leak slowly away.

'I hope we find their kitchen fairly soon,' Pias whispered as they walked.

Yvette's stomach was insistently reminding her that it had been a long time since she, too, had eaten her last meal. But there were priorities to be established. 'First things first. We have to plan for our eventual rescue. Since we can't leave this asteroid to get help, we'll have to ask the help to come to us. For that, I'll need to find their computer and the communications center.'

Pias nodded even though he knew Yvette wouldn't be able to see the gesture in the darkness. She was right – they'd have to send out a call for help before they could think of any more worldly requirements. But he *was* hungry.

Light seeped into the duct from various gratings ahead of them. Looking out, Pias and Yvette found a number of common rooms where the pirates could spend their leisure time. Smaller ducts branched out from the one in which the SOTE agents were walking, probably to individual sleeping quarters, they decided. They continued on their way.

They came to a large room where the crew and other passengers of the *Querida* were being held captive. There were only two guards armed with blasters stationed at the door to oversee better than forty people; with just the blaster they had taken from the pirate they'd killed, Yvette would have been able to eliminate those two guards without even leaving the duct, thereby freeing all their fellow captives. But at the moment that would be a foolish act; she would have to develop a definite plan before tipping her hand so conclusively – otherwise she would have to herd forty people around in enemy territory, with no one knowing what they were doing. She and Pias made a mental note of where this place was, then continued on their travels.

They came to one end of the duct; the corridor branched at right angles to either side of them. Making a decision at random, they took the right-hand tunnel. It was darker than before, with no side gratings to indicate separate rooms. They continued for a long while before they noticed the light at the far end growing brighter. By the time they reached it and gazed out, they were amazed at what they saw.

Just outside the grating was a domed enclosure like the Air Recycling Plant, only smaller. Tools, construction equipment and racks of spacesuits were stacked around the interior, and there was an airlock on the farther side. Outside the transparent dome was a fleet of better than fifty ships. They varied greatly in size and model – small luxury yachts, independent carriers, good-sized cargo vessels – but all looked ready to fly should the order be given.

The two agents backed a little way into the duct to ponder this development. They both knew that ordinary pirates did not need a fleet that big to do their job. They were, for the most part, independent operators who did not work in fleets. One ship, or two at the most, was usually enough for them to accomplish their purpose. After they'd looted a ship, they usually left it floating in space. But these pirates apparently took their catches back to their base and rebuilt them. For what purpose?

'They must be building an army,' Yvette concluded. She explained to Pias about the medallion she had seen around the neck of Ling, the pirate leader, and that she and Jules had learned it was the recognition symbol of important members within an Empire-wide conspiracy. She made no mention of Lady A, saying only that the conspiracy was masterminded by some pretty shrewd operators.

Pias nodded slowly. 'There's no better way to get ships than to steal them, I suppose,' he agreed. 'But where are they going to attack, and when?'

'I don't know, but it's our job to prevent it if at all possible. That's just one more reason why we have to find

114

some way of getting out of this mess – and fast. Let's see what we can find back along the other corridor.'

As they walked back in the other direction, the glimmering of a plan began to form in Yvette's mind. It made beautiful use of everything they'd found so far – these air ducts, the other prisoners, the rebuilt ships. But it was all contingent upon her being able to put in a call for help. They *had* to find the communications center.

They reached the point where the duct had branched off, and this time explored the left-hand tunnel. This led to a more populated portion of the pirate base, and they did indeed locate the kitchen and dining areas. Further on they found what they'd been looking for: a room filled with electronic gadgetry and banks of flashing lights, together with a powerful subcom transmitter/receiver. Unfortunately there were two pirates stationed on duty here at the moment – and the grating separating Pias and Yvette from the outside room was only wide enough for one of them at a time to crawl through.

They conferred for a moment and decided on a plan. Pias waited at the grill with his ministunner all set. The instant one of the men came within range, he fired. The general hum of machines inside the room drowned out the faint buzzing of the stunner; to the other man, it would appear as though his friend had suddenly fainted in the middle of the floor. As he came over to help the fallen pirate, the second man also became a victim of Pias's small but effective weapon. With those two out of commission, Pias quickly slipped off the grate that covered the duct's outlet and he and Yvette invaded the room.

'Stand guard for me,' Yvette said. 'I'll need about half an hour in here. First I have to take some astrogational measurements and figure out exactly where we are, and then I have to call the Circus for help.'

'Why not SOTE or the Navy? They might be closer than your family.'

'No, the Navy is fine when you need muscle, but we've got a situation here that requires a little finesse. Remember, there are forty-some innocent people down here that we'll want to get out alive – including ourselves. The Navy's style would be to bomb this place into insensibility; it would work, but the cost would be high. My family is a little more flexible.'

After stacking the two unconscious pirates in one corner and taking their weapons from them, Pias had nothing to do except watch Yvette go through her complex calculations at the computer. Her exact procedure was a mystery to him. In the four months he had spent at the Service Academy, he had only had time to take the basic indoctrinational courses; he still had no knowledge of the more esoteric fields such as astrogation or spaceship piloting. He made a silent vow, though, as he watched his fiancée work, that he would learn everything he might possibly need to help him perform his job better; he did not enjoy feeling this helpless in a desperate situation.

At last Yvette received the answers she wanted and turned to the subcom unit. 'Let's see,' she said under her breath, 'as I recall the schedule, the Circus should be on Carafia about now. That's not too far away.' And she began the complicated dialing procedure that would allow her to send an instant message to her father's personal subcom receiver.

It took another five minutes before the screen lit up and a three-dimensional image of her father's head appeared. He looked tired and grumpy, as though he'd been awakened late at night – and the odds were good that he had been. 'Who is ... Yvette!' His face lit up as he saw her image on his own screen. 'How are you?'

Yvette had to choose her conversation carefully. There was no scrambler on the subcom she was using, which meant there was always a risk of this call being intercepted. Whatever she said would have to sound innocuous. 'Perfect, Papa. Just perfect.'

Etienne d'Alembert's eyes narrowed just the tiniest crack. The d'Alemberts had a verbal code for communicating when there was a possibility of eavesdropping, and the word 'perfect' meant that things were far from it. His daughter was in trouble and she was calling him for help. Any suggestion of fatigue left his face instantly.

They talked for another five minutes. Although their conversation sounded rambling and sometimes silly to Pias – as it was intended to sound to *any* outsider – an enormous amount of information was exchanged. Yvette managed to tell her father that she was stranded on a pirates' asteroid, and that she was currently free to move about, but couldn't leave. She was able to encode the exact position of the asteroid, and she informed him that there was a fleet of ships on the surface that could conceivably be launched against him. And she told him that there were more than forty people besides herself in need of rescuing.

For his part, Etienne acknowledged her information and replied that he could have a full d'Alembert attack force at the asteroid within four days, and that he would make sure the Navy backed them up, though it would take no part in the actual assault. Yvette assured him she could hold out that long, and told him she loved him. That last part did not need to be encoded. Her father echoed the sentiment and they signed off.

Though Yvette had said all would be smooth, she was far from confident. She and Pias and the other prisoners would have to hold out against the pirates for four days on the latters' home territory. She hoped it could be done.

THE ACCIDENT

The man Howard had hired to arrange Jules's and Vonnie's accident was a professional Howard had used on similar occasions. He knew that their deaths should occur far enough away from Howard's house that suspicion could not possibly fall on the criminal leader. He also knew it should take him long enough to drive to the proper location for Howard to establish a solid alibi. The car in which the accident would occur was a stolen one, so it would not be traceable to anyone connected with Howard's gang when it was found smashed at the bottom of a hillside. All the details had been worked out precisely.

This killer had a favorite spot for his work – an isolated mountain road twenty kilometers from Howard's house. Like many of the mountain roads in Southern California, it had its share of hairpin curves, any one of which had a history of sending motorists to their deaths. The hillside below the road was thick with underbrush, so the car might remain unnoticed for hours or days, if all went well. And there was a nearby hiking trail that the killer could take to walk down the mountainside and be back within the limits of civilization in an hour and a half, from which point he could call a cab to get him home.

The man was concentrating so much on the details of this accident that he failed to notice Vonnie's slight stirring in the back seat. The shock she had received from Howard's burglar deterrent system had been a strong one, and had kept her unconscious for a long time; but she was young and in perfect health, and her DesPlainian constitution allowed her to overcome the effects of the shock slightly faster than might be expected of anyone else. She began to regain consciousness just as Howard's henchman was nearing the spot he had selected for the double murder.

At first her mind was clouded as it struggled back toward reality. She remembered the shock from the windowsill, and the consternation she had felt over committing such an amateurish mistake. Now she could tell that she was lying down in a moving vehicle. Someone else's body was lying

118

beside hers, also unconscious, but at first she had trouble focusing her eyes to see who it was. She continued to lie very still, however. She realized that, whatever the situation, those around her expected her to still be unconscious; she would be able to learn more if they continued to believe that.

When her eyes began to work properly once more, she could see that the body beside her was Jules, and that he was also unconscious or pretending to be so. This alarmed her considerably. She and Jules were working alone on this case; for them both to be captured at once meant they had no one to back them up or pull them out of trouble. The fact that they were bundled in the back seat of a car and were being driven somewhere was an ominous sign.

At about the time she reached this conclusion, the car pulled to a stop. Vonnie quickly closed her eyes once more to feign unconsciousness. She could hear the front door opening as the driver got out and opened the back door. The man grabbed her under the arms and dragged her out, positioning her in the front seat on the passenger side. Vonnie 'cooperated' by pretending to be a limp body, and she slumped forward obligingly when he let go of her until her forehead rested lightly against the dashboard.

As the man returned to the back seat for Jules, Vonnie was computing the odds for and against various plans. The driver's intentions were obvious by now – placing her and Jules in the front seat unconscious could only be the set-up for a groundcar accident in which their deaths would be untraceable to Howard. She obviously did not want it to succeed – but the exact method for foiling it was debatable.

There was only the one man to deal with, and he still thought she was out cold. She would have little trouble overpowering him and freeing herself and Jules if she chose to do so. But the man might be expected to report back to Howard; if he failed to check in, the criminal leader would know something had gone wrong. Being thus alerted might panic him into doing something rash.

It would be very convenient to have him think that she and Jules were dead. It would put him off his guard to the point where he might grow careless. In order to do that, she would have to let the killer carry out his attempt and think it had succeeded. This course of action would be much more difficult, and would require split-second timing and a little bit of luck on top of it – but the rewards would be well worth the gamble.

Vonnie continued her pretense of unconsciousness as the killer dumped Jules's body into the driver's seat beside her. Then, giving them a quick look to make sure they were both unconscious, the man closed the door and went to the back of the car. He gave it a strong push, and Vonnie could feel the car moving forward. Her right hand crept to the doorhandle while her left went over to grab Jules's clothing. If he really was still out, she wanted to take him with her when she jumped.

She could feel the car bump as it went over an embankment, and suddenly it was plunging downward through dense clumps of bushes. To someone born of Earth, the fall would have been at a dizzying speed, but to a person with DesPlainian reflexes it was almost slow motion. Vonnie waited two seconds, until she hoped she was far enough out of sight that the killer would not be able to see exactly what was happening to the car. Then, in a quick series of motions, she sprang into action.

Her right arm pushed against the car door. There was some resistance as the heavy brush around the car resisted her attempt to open the door, but Vonnie was pressing with the strength of a DesPlainian – and a desperate DesPlainian, at that. The door opened. With her left hand she grabbed her fiancé's jacket collar and pulled him over to her. Then, before the underbrush that was sliding past at an ever increasing rate could push the door shut again, she leaped out of the moving vehicle, taking Jules with her.

The two bodies rolled free in the overgrown vegetation. Vonnie felt herself banging into rocks and catching on branches and brambles, leaving her skin with a rich assortment of bruises and scratches. Jules's body tumbled beside her until the underbrush had provided enough resistance to stop their fall. Vonnie lay still for more than a minute, panting to regain her breath.

Below them, the car continued to charge down the hillside like a stampeding bull elephant, gathering momentum as it flew. A hundred meters beyond the point at which

Vonnie and Jules had left it, the car encountered a tree stump that caused it to flip over without otherwise stopping the downhill charge. The car began bouncing crazily through the air; in landed upside-down on a large, outcropping boulder, causing the metal of the roof to buckle inward. Any bodies that might have been seated in there would have been crushed to death at that point. And still the car continued to bounce three more times before coming to rest, a battered hulk, near the bottom of the ravine.

Vonnie gave a small sigh of relief that she had managed to pull herself and Jules out in time. Even after she had completely regained her breath, however, she moved very carefully. Reorienting her body, she looked upward to the top of the hill, hoping for some sight of the man who'd tried to kill her. It was difficult to both see and remain hidden at the same time, and the angle of her view was working against her; she thought she could make out a face peering down from the road for a few seconds, but then it vanished. As the echoing sound of the car's crash died away, a bucolic stillness settled once more over the mountainside.

Vonnie crept slowly through the bushes and weeds to the spot where Jules lay, some three meters away. 'Julie?' she whispered, but got no answer. Bending over him, she could tell that his breathing was light but irregular. She felt for his pulse; it was reassuringly strong and steady. When she lifted his eyelids, she could see that his pupils were mere pinpoints and that the whites of his eyes were slightly bloodshot. All these were effects of a stun-gun hit; but how severely he had been jolted, she couldn't tell.

She debated what to do. The fact that the killer hadn't come down here after her proved that he was satisfied he'd done his job successfully; he wouldn't want to hang around the scene of this accident too long, or someone might come by and associate him with it. The immediate threat from him was over. But there was still the unknown damage to Jules that worried her considerably. The stun he'd gotten must have been at least a four, which would put him out for two hours. But if it were any higher he could be out for days, or even permanently paralyzed – and in that case, she couldn't just let him lie here. She'd have to get some help.

But she didn't want to leave him alone here, either, if she could avoid it.

She decided to wait with him for another hour or so. If it had only been a number four stun, he would start to snap out of it by that time; if it had been anything higher, he would be out for at least another four hours beyond that, which would give her time to bring back help before he awoke and needed her.

She stood up and stretched her stiff, sore body, walking around for a while to get the kinks out and trying to discover any way of getting back to the city. She noticed a hiking trail a short distance away, but she could also tell that it was late in the afternoon; she might not have the time to walk along the trail to civilization and still return for Jules before the sun went down – and she'd hate to have to try to find his body in the dark. Returning to him, she sat down beside him, cradling his head in her lap and smiling down at his handsome face. She waited for something to happen.

After forty-five minutes Jules began rolling his head slightly from side to side, and within another five he was coughing and trying to open his eyes. 'Take it easy,' Vonnie said, stroking his forehead with a light touch of her fingertips. 'You're just coming out of stun. There's no immediate danger, so take your time.'

'Howard ... ambushed me,' Jules explained a few moments later as he got his tongue back into operation. 'He must be onto us.'

'Not any more. He thinks we're dead now.' She explained the events that had happened since she herself had regained consciousness.

By the time she finished, Jules was able to pull himself up weakly into a sitting position. He gave Vonnie a wobbly smile and said, 'Thanks for saving my life.'

She reached over and ruffled his already-mussed brown hair. 'Don't worry; I have some future plans for you that don't include letting Howard kill you.'

As soon as Jules was steady enough to stand, the two DesPlainians climbed up the hill to the road; Vonnie decided that there was more chance of their being able to hitch a ride there than there was of walking down the hiking trail before it got dark. As they climbed, they were already turning their minds back to the case on which they were working.

'The wedding is scheduled for tomorrow afternoon,' Jules said, 'and Howard is assembling his gang in the morning. We don't have to be as smart as the Head to figure out that the two events are connected. There isn't a hell of a lot of time left between now and then. We'd be cutting it very fine, and I don't like taking chances like that with the lives of the Imperial family. I'm almost tempted to arrest Howard now and to hell with the consequences. It could very well be that his absence will be enough to wreck the conspiracy's plans.'

'Except that you don't really believe that, do you?' Vonnie's eyes gleamed back at him in the late afternoon sunlight.

'No, I don't. They've shown themselves to be pretty resourceful so far. Either they have a contingency plan already in mind or else they'd know we were onto them and disappear into the woodwork for a while – and Bozhe only knows what nasty little surprises they'd dream up for us next time. We have to try to stop them here and now.'

They made it back up to the highway and, after a quarter of an hour, managed to hitch a ride with a young man driving into the city. Their benefactor took them to a vidicom booth where they were able to summon a cab. The taxi drove them first back to the area near Howard's house where Vonnie had left their car parked; it was still at the same spot, undiscovered by Howard. While she stayed there to continue her surveillance of Howard's house, Jules continued on in the cab back to their hotel, where he would prepare for his own action of the evening.

Howard's gang would be reassembling tomorrow morning to receive their instructions. Now that Howard thought his opposition was eliminated, he would be unlikely to alter those plans. If Jules was no longer going to be an invited guest at the gathering, he intended to be an uninvited one.

Gathering his gear together – including a small personal com unit linked to the one in the car, so he could maintain constant communications with Vonnie – he grabbed a quick snack from the food machines in the hotel lobby and took a cab to the vicinity of Howard's gym. It was full night by the time he reached it, but the interior of the gym was brightly lit; if it kept standard hours, there would be customers inside there until close to midnight. Jules roamed the streets around the neighborhood until the gym was finally closed, then went to work.

The building next to the gym was an apartment house. Jules entered it and took the elevator tube to the top floor, then located the emergency stairway to the roof. From there it was a simple matter to jump the two-meter gap that separated the apartment building from the gym. On the roof of his objective, Jules fastened a sturdy carlon line and lowered himself over the edge until he was standing on the ledge beside the top row of windows. A quick check with his sophisticated sensors revealed that the alarms used here were of the simplest variety, and it was the work of less than a minute to bypass them altogether. One window wasn't even locked; Jules pried it open and slipped into the darkened building.

The room he'd entered was an auxiliary office – rarely used, to judge by the dust that lay thickly on the surfaces of the furniture. The rest of the building sounded quite still and Jules slipped quietly out the office door and padded down the darkened hallway. The gym itself contained little of value and Howard had seen no need to put a guard on it, so Jules was able to prowl unhindered throughout the large building until he came to the room that was marked as Howard's private office.

Inside, he went straight to the vidicom set and installed the same sort of bug that Vonnie had attempted to place on Howard's home phone earlier. He also stuck a tiny transmitter on the underside of Howard's desk, so that any conversations taking place within this office could be monitored. Then he went down the hall to the other meeting room, such as the one in which he'd had his briefing, and made sure that they were all bugged as well. He was going to take no chances on missing the plan that Howard described to his men. He even planted transmitters in the 'freshers, just to be on the safe side.

When he was absolutely certain that not even a sneeze would escape without detection, he set about to find him self a suitable hiding place. He found a janitor's closet on the upper floor that fitted his qualifications admirably and, tucking himself in among the mops and pails, he sat down to await results. On his private com unit, he called Vonnie and learned that all was quiet at Howard's house. She would let him know the instant anything happened.

Thus assured, Jules settled himself down to rest before the big showdown. His sleep was far from peaceful, though, as he realized exactly how slender was the margin within which he and Vonnie were operating.

Vonnie woke him early to let him know that Howard had left the house and was on his way into town, presumably to the gym. She would follow him at a discreet distance and, when he came to the gym, she would wait outside to give Jules any help he might require. Jules checked his microphones one final time to make sure they were all working, and prepared himself for the ordeal he knew today would prove to be.

Vonnie informed him, finally, that Howard had just entered the gym, and that she was parked across the street. A few minutes later, Jules could pick out the sounds of Howard entering the office and sitting at the desk, going through papers. At precisely nine-thirty, the vidicom buzzed and Howard quickly picked it up. Jules switched on his recording device and listened in at the same time.

'Phase One is now accomplished,' said the feminine voice at the other end without preamble. With a chill down his spine, Jules recognized that voice as belonging to Lady A. 'Bloodstar Hall is now ours. We control all the access to it, and no communication can get through our interference pattern, not even SOTE's. Once we start moving we can seal the entire place off until we're ready to announce the outcome ourselves.'

Howard gave a slow whistle of appreciation. 'How did you manage that?'

Jules could not intercept the video transmission on his device, but he could imagine Lady A giving Howard one of her coldly superior smiles. 'We have a ... shall we say, a cooperative *double* of Lady Bloodstar – a perfect lookalike who has moved in and assumed the role ... at the expense of the real one, of course. Have you memorized the guard positions and the different strike points I gave you?'

'Yes, Your Ladyship.'

'Good. At precisely one minute past noon, our double will make her move. It will cause confusion within the hall sufficient for our purposes. At the same time, ten small cannisters of TCN-14 will be exploding outside the hall eliminating the guards there. Your men, in gas masks, will move in effortlessly and take up the positions of the fallen SOTE guards; they will therefore be in a perfect position to control the immediate area. SOTE picked those spots very carefully for their maximum effectiveness, and we'll make them work to *our* advantage. If all goes well, we'll have effected a complete coup in just under ten minutes. And I assure you, my dear Gospodin Howard, that your part in it will not go unrewarded.' Without waiting for further acknowledgement Lady A cut off the call.

Jules was horror-stricken as he listened to the plans. Although Lady A had been most circumspect in telling Howard about the 'double' she had for Lady Bloodstar, Jules could guess instantly the double's true nature – a robot. He and Vonnie had already faced a sample of this particular kind of menace once before, on the planet Ansegria. There, a robot who looked and acted exactly like a specific person had been set as a trap to ensnare the Crown Princess Edna. SOTE had learned that there were at least three more such robots loose somewhere in the Empire, though their appearances and their missions had remained a mystery. Now, in at least one case, that mystery was solved. One robot was a duplicate of Lady Bloodstar.

The fact that Lady A's organization would be using cannisters of TCN-14 outside the hall was an ominous sign, too. Trichloronoluene was a deadly nerve gas developed in pre-Empire times, when individual planets could – and did, with astonishing frequency – make war upon each other. The TCN spread out from its source in a noxious green cloud, and a single whiff was lethal; whole cities had been known to succumb to it as it rained down in explosive cannisters from spaceships orbiting a hostile world. One historian had even gone so far as to say that it was TCN-14, rather than economic or political causes, that had made the Empire necessary; there *had* to be peace between the planets, because the alternative was simply too unthinkable.

If Lady A were using TCN-14 merely to eliminate some guards and keep the populace from getting out of hand during her takeover, then her regime obviously would be conducting its business in the most coldblooded way possible.

Vonnie's voice came over his com unit, breaking him out of his horrified reverie. 'We're getting company. Looks like some of our blasterbats are arriving.'

'We'll wait until they're all in, then make our haul,' Jules said between very tight lips. Then, as succinctly as he could, he outlined the conspiracy's plan to topple the Empire.

Vonnie listened very quietly. Jules knew that quiet mood of hers – it was a rage beyond words, being directed at Lady A and her minions, and he pitied them a little. He himself would rather have a dozen people ranting at him than have Vonnie go suddenly quiet like that.

'We'll get them,' was all she said – but her tone spoke volumes.

The hour of ten o'clock came and the men were all assembled in the designated meeting room. Monitoring via his microphones, Jules could hear their restless stirring, becoming suddenly quiet as Howard entered the room. 'Now that we're all here,' the criminal leader said, 'we can begin.'

That was Jules's cue. 'We move in now,' he said tersely to Vonnie. 'Give me two minutes to start some confusion, then come in and help me mop up.'

He left his closet and ran down the hall to the fire detector. Aiming his blaster at the spot on the wall just below the thermocouple, he shot out a narrow beam of high intensity. The sensor in the wall, detecting the sudden increase in temperature near it, immediately sent in the alarm to the local fire station. At the same time, it began a series of high-pitched wails echoing down the corridors of the old gymnasium building.

The alarm did indeed cause confusion in the ranks of the

men who'd come to hear Howard's orders. Some sat open-mouthed in their chairs, not knowing what to do. Others looked to Howard for his reaction. A handful more panicked, getting up from their seats and running out of the room.

In doing so, they moved straight from the frying pan into the fire – Jules's fire. The SOTE agent cut them down like targets in a shooting gallery with a rapidfire series of stungun bolts. Within a mere ten seconds, six of his adversaries were lying unconscious on the floor, and the fight hadn't even begun.

By now the automatic sprinkling system had turned on, and water mixed with fire extinguishing foam was spraying forcefully from all the ceilings in the building. Everyone – Jules as well as the gangsters – was soaked as the building tried to defend itself from the supposed menace. The footing was treacherous from the slippery fluids, but Jules did not much care – this was one fight he intended to win effortlessly.

Sliding into the meeting room, his first shot went straight at Howard. Then, with a deft spin like a ballet dancer, he turned and directed his stun-gun fire around the room. Most of the men were too surprised to even reach for their guns before Jules's bolts hit home. Those who made at least an attempt to reach for their own weapons still were no match for Jules's DesPlainian reflexes.

By the time Vonnie raced into the building, gun drawn, there was nothing left for her to do. She slogged her way through the water and foam, which was ankle deep in some places, until she reached her fiancé's side, 'I guess you really meant it when you said you needed me to mop up.'

But Jules had no time for even the most basic of humor. 'These thugs won't be going anywhere for a while,' he said, taking Vonnie by the arm and leading her back toward the front door. 'The fire department can take care of them until the crisis is over. We have more important things to do.'

There were less than two hours before Lady A's plans were to go into effect. Jules only hoped that would be enough time.

CHAPTER ELEVEN

BATTLE FOR THE PIRATE ASTEROID

As Yvette began explaining her plan to Pias, she repeatedly emphasized the crucial ingredient of timing. 'Everything has to be coordinated. We have to take each step in order and we have to make sure the others know what they're supposed to do, or the whole thing goes up in smoke.'

Pias nodded. Being responsible for the safety of the more than forty people from their ship under circumstances like these was not an enviable task. Yvette's plan was deceptively simple – and in its simplicity lay the one hope they had that it would work. 'I'm ready to try it if you are.'

Yvette turned, pulled her blaster and sprayed its fiery beam over the communications and computer room. The pirates would learn soon enough that they had been here; if the equipment were left intact, they might be able to guess some of what really happened. It would be better to give them the impression that the escapees were only interested in producing random damage to a vital area of the base. And besides, it *would* lead to some confusion and diminution of the pirates' abilities to act.

As they'd thought, the use of the blaster within this nerve center of the base touched off a series of alarm bells that they could hear ringing far in the distance. 'Now we've got to move,' Pias said.

'And you know where,' his fiancée agreed.

They slipped back into the air vent and closed the grating behind them. Retracing their path quickly down the darkened tunnel, they returned to the outlet that fed the room where their fellow passengers from the *Querida* were kept prisoner. The alarm bells were ringing here, too, and everyone – captive and pirate alike – was uncertain what would happen. The two guards had their blasters drawn and ready to fire at the least suspicious movement from the prisoners.

From her vantage point behind the grill, Yvette opened fire on the guards. Both men dropped instantly as the searing beam from her blaster raked through them. Passengers screamed as this new and unexpected development occurred. They were sure it would be their turn next, and they looked around wildly to see what direction the shots had come from and how they might be able to defend themselves.

Pias quickly undid the grating and slithered into the room, with Yvette right behind him. It took their friends a frenzied second before they recognized their saviors, but a loud cheer rang out from two score of throats.

Pias held up his hands for silence. 'Quiet! We're not safe yet – and if you ever want to be, you'll have to follow my instructions *exactly*. There isn't time for questions.' Although it was Yvette's plan, they had both agreed that he would be the one to appear the leader; it might instill a trifle more confidence in the unenlightened.

'Someone take the blasters from those two guards,' Pias said. 'They won't need them any more, and we certainly will. Who here knows how to use them?'

Several hands went up, and there was a quick division of their weaponry. There were now five captured blasters plus Pias's ministunner; Yvette kept the blaster she'd been using and gave a second to the *Querida*'s Captain Bacardi, whom she then took aside and spoke to in private. As Pias gave out two more blasters to members of the ship's crew, keeping the last one for himself, he watched the captain nod silent agreement and slip off into the ventilating duct with Yvette.

Pias took a deep breath. For the next half hour or so he'd be on his own. This would be a test of exactly how much leadership ability he had.

'Our next stop,' Pias bellowed, making sure everyone could hear him, 'is the kitchen.'

'Why the kitchen?' one man asked.

'We'll need supplies if we're going to last for the next four days,' Pias said impatiently. 'And the longer I have to stand here explaining, the less time we'll have to act. The pirates won't be expecting us to hit the supplies – they probably think we're so scared we'll head straight for a ship. Let's go, on the double. And if you see anyone who isn't one of us, attack first and ask questions later.'

They burst out into the hallway, where the alarms were sounding even louder. No one else was in sight at the moment, so Pias led his party down the narrow corridors to the supply pantry. Although the route was strange to him, his knowledge of the way the ventilating shafts went allowed him to find his destination.

At one point a trio of pirates crossed their path at an intersection. They were surprised to see the prisoners traveling freely down the halls, but the surprise was short-lived – as were, in fact, the pirates thimselves. The Newforester blasted them down without mercy in a single sweep of his gun, and his group continued on.

The larder, not being considered a crucial spot, had been left unguarded during this emergency. Pias left two men at the door to serve as his own guards, then went into the storage area with the rest of his escapees. He spent the next fifteen minutes frantically directing his people which things would be best to take along and which would be best to leave.

'We'll need supplies for four days,' he kept repeating. 'Empty those containers over there and fill them with water. Lots of fluids, that's what we'll need primarily. Liquid is bulky and hard to carry, so we have to devote most of our energies that way. Get some of the smaller, more compact foodstuffs – no, not those cans, we might not be able to open them. Hurry, every second is precious!'

When at last everyone was properly encumbered, Pias ordered another move-out. They were a little behind his estimated time schedule and he knew Yvette would be waiting desperately for him. He had to herd his group to the room that led to the spaceship docks, and he had to hope that Yvette had been able to carry out her end of the plan.

While Pias had been preparing the prisoners for the march on the pantry, Yvette had taken Captain Bacardi aside. 'While they're off getting supplies,' she said, 'you and I have another job. We've got to steal a ship big enough to hold all of us. I know where their dockyards are. Come with me.'

The captain nodded and slipped into the ventilating shaft at Yvette's heels. The DesPlainian led him to the outlet into the ship room. Several pirates were now stationed here at their emergency posts. 'We'll have to get rid of them before we can do anything else,' she said. Patting her own blaster, she added, 'I hope you're not squeamish about using one of these.'

Captain Bacardi nodded and tightened his grip on the blaster she'd given him. 'Nothing's too much to use on these vermin,' he said. 'I watched pirates space half my crew once. They won't get any mercy from me.'

'This isn't a vendetta, either,' Yvette warned. 'We just want them out of the way as efficiently as possible. As soon as they're eliminated we put on spacesuits from the rack over there and go out to steal ourselves a ship. Understood?'

'Smooth,' the captain nodded.

Yvette unfastened the grating and with a sudden violent kick sent it flying across the room. The startled pirates within the dome looked up and their attention was held for several seconds by the anomalous flight of the ventilator grill over their heads. By the time they could think of anything else, it was too late.

Yvette and the captain emerged from their tunnel, prepared for a fight but also braced with caution. The room they were in was a transparent dome, with the deadly vacuum of space on the other side. Though the dome's material was tough enough to withstand even micrometeoroid impacts, a stray blaster beam could prove disastrous. It did not fit in with Yvette's plans to puncture the dome and destroy the entire pirate base by explosive decompression.

Therefore, the two attackers did not fire at random as they might otherwise have done. They took their time to aim carefully at the surprised pirates, and each shot they placed was true. By the time the defenders could draw their weapons, the fight was essentially over; they themselves hesitated to risk a wild shot that might damage the dome over their heads, and the fraction of a second their indecision cost them was sufficient. Yvette and the captain were left alone in the dome.

With the fighting over for the moment, the captain looked outside at the crowded spaceport field. '*Bozhe moi!*' he exclaimed. 'They've got a whole navy of their own out there.'

Yvette had already gone to the racks that held scores of

spacesuits and took one that was approximately her size. As she quickly clambered into it, she said, 'Yes. Pick one that will hold all our people and let's get moving. Whatever ship you pick will have to be lifting off in half an hour.'

The long but necessary delay at the food lockers gave the pirates time to zero in on the location of Pias's group. As they made their way out toward the spaceship dock, the people from the *Querida* encountered much more resistance. Twice they were pinned down by enemy fire before they were able to kill their antagonists and move on. Three of the ship's company were cut down by blaster fire in the densely packed hallways. But Pias did manage to shepherd almost the entire contingent safely into the spacedock dome and barricaded the door behind them by moving some heavy equipment into place against it. It would take the pirates at least twenty minutes to get through.

There was no sign of Yvette and the captain, but Pias refused to wait. 'Everyone take a spacesuit,' he called, pointing at the racks to one side of the dome. 'It doesn't matter whether it's your size or not – you won't be wearing it, anyway.'

A woman beside him gave him a startled glance. 'Then how are we supposed to get out to the ships?'

As Pias followed her gesture with his eyes, he could make out two spacesuited figures loping across the spaceport field back toward the dome. That would be Yvette and the captain – or, at least, he hoped it was.

'We don't go out to the ships,' was Pias's soft reply. 'We stay nice and cozy in there—' he pointed at the hole in the wall that led to the system of ventilator ducts '—while we wait to be rescued four days from now.'

There were rumblings of mutiny in the ranks, and many of the passengers were uncertain of the wisdom of Pias's plan. The arrival of the two spacesuited people at the airlock forestalled any questioning; they indeed turned out to be Yvette and Captain Bacardi, and they added their influence to that of Pias. Slowly, and with not a little grumbling, the passengers from the *Querida* complied with their orders. Each took a spacesuit from the racks and carried it with him into the air shafts.

'I still don't see why we don't just take a ship and escape,' one passenger muttered.

Yvette overheard him and merely smiled. 'You will,' she said.

When everyone was back inside the shaft, Yvette and Pias fastened the grating back into place over the hole in the wall. Instead of herding them all away, however, they decided to stick around this area and let people see what happened next. Pias selected three of the top grumblers and made sure they had a good vantage point beside the grill to observe firsthand the events of the next few minutes.

With a trembling that shook the walls around them, even this far away from the scene, the ship that Captain Bacardi had picked lifted off the ground toward the sky. Once the vessel had left the ground the trembling stopped, but the ship continued to rise silently. The departure was slow at first, but as the ship moved further from the planet's surface its determination to escape seemed to increase exponentially. It had been programmed on automatic pilot to blast as far and as fast as possible, and it was trying its best to obey the instructions.

It had gone less than a kilometer from its launching site when suddenly it exploded in a flash of brilliance. There was, of course, no sound in the emptiness of space; one second the ship was a dull form disappearing into the blackness, the next it was a new star blinding the viewers with its intensity. Those who had been watching at the grill pulled back quickly, knuckling their eyes. 'What happened?' someone asked.

'The pirates weren't about to let us get away,' Yvette said quietly. 'They'd rather see us dead than allow us to get back to civilization and tell the authorities the location of this base. Their defensive armament around this asteroid could easily knock any of those ships out of the sky – and that's what they did. We would never have had a chance to escape. Our only hope is to wait here for four days; help is already on the way.'

'But they'll find us and kill us!' one woman cried.

Pias tried to give her a comforting smile, but the gesture

was lost in the darkness of the tunnel. He had to settle, instead, for a calm tone that he hoped would allay her fears. 'No, that's the beauty of this plan. Look at all these events from the pirates' point of view. They know Yvette and I overpowered the guard who'd been taking us to our death. We got away from him and found the rest of you. We all broke out and went to the food locker, where we picked up some supplies to take with us during our escape. Then we came to the spacedock dome, took spacesuits and *apparently* boarded that ship. It took off and was shot down. As far as they're concerned, we're all dead now, and that's the end of the matter. If we stay quiet and inconspicuous, they'll never think to look for us in here. We just have to be careful not to attract their attention.'

They started to settle into a boring, quiet routine. They had sufficient air, food and water, and there was plenty of room for them to move around in to ward off a feeling of claustrophobia. The worst problem figured to be toilet facilities, and even that was taken care of satisfactorily. Yvette had been planning to use one end of the shaft, where there was a slight dip near the Air Recycling Plant, as a drainage trough – uncomfortable, perhaps, but preferable to discovery. But as Pias was going past some of the private quarters, he overheard two pirates talking on the other side of the grill. That particular room had belonged to a pirate who'd died during the fighting with the passengers; his personal effects were being removed and divided up among the rest of his fellows, after which the room would be vacant until a new pirate was recruited. When they left, Pias removed the grating and slid into the room through the small opening in the wall. Bolting the door from the inside made it perfectly safe for their use. One 'fresher for forty people was less than ideal, but it was certainly better than nothing.

Time dragged by with immeasurable slowness, and they dared not even engage in any long conversations to ease the boredom. For the most part, people just sat on the smooth metal floor of the air duct, occasionally standing and walking around to keep their muscles from tightening. Most of the passengers seemed resigned to their fate, and spent their time just sleeping.

Pias and Yvette were nervous at the unaccustomed in activity. Like tigers in a cage they prowled restlessly up and down the tunnel, spying on the daily activities of these pirates. They paid particular attention to the doings of the pirate leader, Ling. He seemed almost as edgy as they were snarling irritably at his men, performing his administrative duties in a foul temper, pacing around the partially des troyed communications room like a man expecting an important message any minute. The two SOTE agents de cided he must be awaiting some orders from his superiors in this conspiracy.

On the morning of the third day after their escape Yvette and Pias heard one of the com officers deliver a verbal message to his commander. 'Message relayed from C sir,' the man said. 'The impostors have all arrived as plan ned, and will be in the hall to take up their positions at the necessary time. If the coup goes well, you'll be given your orders to move in about twenty-four hours, but you are not to make any move at all until you receive the word.'

'More standing and waiting, damn it!' Ling spat angrily. 'It's driving me crazy. Smooth, tell C that I acknowledge his instructions ... but I don't have to enjoy them. Don't, of course, tell him that.'

The two SOTE agents, listening in secret, had gotten an earful. The word 'coup' had put them instantly on their toes, but they were powerless to do anything more than speculate at present. The reference to the 'impostors' puzzled them until, after talking over in quiet whispers with the passengers, they learned that each of them had had personal identification taken away – rings, ID cards, et cetera.

'That's why they had a copy of the passenger list,' Pias said. 'They're going to impersonate all the nobility that was aboard the *Querida*. But how can they hope to get away with an impersonation like that? The computers should be able to spot the frauds in a second.'

'It's possible to make exact robot doubles of people,' Yvette told him. 'Jules and I already ran across one that was frighteningly perfect.'

'There were thirty nobles on the passenger list. Could they make that many robots?'

'I don't know. Jules and I have only learned about three more on the loose – and two of those were made to look like people from high-grav worlds, which wouldn't match any of these passengers at all. They apparently are very difficult machines to construct, but even so this conspiracy is well financed ... I'd have to think about it some more.'

'That mention of twenty-four hours – it must refer to the Princess's wedding. That's scheduled for tomorrow.'

'I know.' Yvette slumped down to a sitting position against the wall. 'It all makes me feel so impotent, knowing something's going to happen and being unable to do anything.'

Pias gave her a smile. 'We have an old saying on New-forest : "You can't steal a chicken while wearing boxing gloves." '

'What's that supposed to mean?'

'It means that the first thing you have to do is take off the gloves. We've got gloves on right now, and we can't do anything else until we get them off – which won't be until your family rescues us tomorrow. Besides, your brother's on Earth – he's probably already got everything well in hand.'

Yvette did not tell Pias about one other thing that was worrying her – this new factor of a boss known only as 'C'. How did he relate to Lady A in the conspiracy's hierarchy? Was he her boss, her equal or her subordinate? And did the existence of an A and C also indicate the possibility of a 'B' running around somewhere behind the scenes?

There were no answers to her questions, and she dared not risk breaking the cover of all the people here just to find a little more information. She could only hope her father would get here soon and rescue them so that they could send the news about the attempted coup back to Earth as fast as possible.

The attack, when it did come, was so skillfully done that it was halfway over before the pirates even realized it was occurring. The big Circus ship emerged from subspace more than a full lightsecond away from the pirates' asteroid –

well out of its detection range. It launched a projectile at its target that looked like merely another rock, a piece of space debris no more than a dozen meters in diameter. Because the rock was so small, and because it had no means of self-propulsion for the pirates' sensors to detect, it failed to activate the automatic alarm system. The course it was travelling would take it no closer than a hundred meters from the base, so there was seemingly no reason for concern.

However, shortly before the rock reached its nearest point to the asteroid, it burst apart and ejected a score of figures clad in space battle armor. Like the tiny car that pulls into the center of the circus ring and disgorges limitless numbers of clowns, the rock had been packed full of d'Alemberts waiting for just the proper moment to emerge. Activating small airjets on their suits, they rocketed silently down to the surface of the asteroid without giving the inhabitants the slightest notice of their existence.

Another rock flew past shortly behind the first. This one also sprang apart to release its contents: a few more members of the d'Alembert clan as well as all the equipment the invading force would need. These, too, were jetted down to the surface without detection.

Now the invaders were ready to get to work. Three of them separated and went to the outside gun emplacements. Once the fighting started on other fronts, the pirates would not be paying attention to more alarms ringing; it would then be the job of these three to dismantle the automatic blasters that guarded the asteroid, so that the Circus ship and its naval companion could come in closer and use their own weaponry to aid in the battle.

The rest of the d'Alemberts clustered around the four main airlocks of the pirate base. With them they had small boarding hatches, identical in concept with the ones the pirates themselves had used to break into the Querida. These people were used to working as a team, as they regularly put up the Circus's tents wherever they played. Within a matter of only a few seconds, the attack was ready to begin in earnest.

Alarm bells started ringing within the base as the d'Alemberts applied their cutting torches to the outside of the airlocks. They wasted little time with formality; they were through the outer walls before most of the pirates even realized precisely what was going on. The defenders had little time to get into their own battle armor before the fighting was underway.

Soon the major corridors were sizzling with energy as blaster bolts were beaming up and down their length. As the d'Alembert forces poured in from four different entrances at once, pockets of defenders found themselves cut off and isolated from their comrades. The d'Alemberts, for their part, were merciless in exterminating anyone who showed even the least bit of resistance.

Alarms were also ringing in the central control room, indicating that the big exterior blasters were being tampered with. In the general confusion, however, none of the pirates noticed this development until it was far too late to do anything about it.

Some pirates blockaded their sections, hoping to stall for time and get into their own battle armor to fight back against these unknown invaders – but they found themselves unexpectedly attacked from a new direction. Blaster bolts coming out of the air shafts struck them down from behind as Pias's and Yvette's forces took advantage of the confusion to assist in their own rescue. The pirates now did not know which way to turn – even the safest directions were suddenly fraught with unknown peril.

A few of the pirates decided that flight might be the safest alternative – but even that avenue was blocked. As they ran in their spacesuits across the landing field where their ships were docked, they were frozen in their tracks by the sight of an Imperial battle cruiser looming overhead – just a bit of extra backup Duke Etienne had called for at the last moment. The Navy gunners had a fine day of target practice, destroying all the pirate ships on the ground before even a single one of them could take to the ether. Within an hour from the moment the battle had started, the pirates were beaming out an urgent message of surrender.

With the cessation of hostilities, Yvette led the passengers of the *Querida* out into the open once more and remanded them to the custody of the naval officers who had landed and were establishing martial order. She herself took Pias by the hand and went with the rest of her relatives back to the Circus ship, which had landed near the battle cruiser.

As soon as they'd peeled off their spacesuits, the two were ushered into the presence of Duke Etienne. The Manager of the Circus embraced his daughter lovingly, then looked over at the man with her. Pias, who had made a point of bringing his hat along, took it off and swept it across his chest as he made a deep bow to his future father-in-law. 'I am honored, Your Grace, to make the acquaintance of a person so distinguished as yourself. The progenitor of such a wonderful daughter is a man worth envying.'

The Duke smiled and turned to Yvette. 'I like him already – he has almost as high an opinion of me as I do.'

Yvette smiled, too, but she did not forget her duty. 'I'm glad, Papa, but right now there's still some more business for us. We've got to send a subcom call to the Head at once. Pias and I overheard some of Ling's plans – there's going to be a coup attempt during the Princess's wedding.'

The Duke looked grimly down at his watch and made a quick mental calculation. 'It may already be too late,' he said. 'According to everything I know about it, the ceremony was supposed to start half an hour ago.'

CHAPTER TWELVE

THE AFFAIR AT BLOODSTAR HALL

Bloodstar Hall was steeped in centuries of tradition. Located in Angeles–Diego, construction had begun on the mammoth structure in 2004. It was called, at the time, the Angels' Palace, and it was being built as a rival to the Houston Astrodome, the New Orleans Superdome and other megalithic sports structures of the day. The political turmoil of the period, however, delayed its completion for years, and it was not until 2028, well into the reign of King Boris I of Earth, that the Angels' Palace was opened to the public.

Although it defied many of the architectural conventions of its day, the Angels' Palace was subsequently called one of the most marvelous planet-based structures built by Man. The exterior was a deliberate return to the massive stonework of the medieval craftsmen, though on a scale those worthies would scarcely have considered. Fluted columns stood by enormous gateways of bronze; massive bas-reliefs depicting key scenes from the history of western civilization surrounded the upper levels; and almost everywhere one looked were carved stone figures lovingly etched into the naked stone.

Inside, the Angels' Palace was equally impressive, completely covered over by a dome of restful blue in which golden 'clouds' drifted at random. With all the seats in, it had a capacity of more than two hundred thousand; remove the seats and nearly half again as many could be packed inside without discomfort. It was the largest structure of its kind ever attempted by Man, and easily one of the wonders of the modern world.

Little wonder that King Stanley VI of Earth chose the Angels' Palace on February 28, 2225 as the spot from which he proclaimed himself Emperor Stanley I of the Empire of Earth. As the message was beamed out to all the planets, the majesty of the new Emperor's surroundings lent even more respectability and authority to the unheard-of grab for power he was making.

And in only five years' time, the Angels' Palace saw an

entirely different usage. The so-called Dukes' Revolt was raging against the Emperor's authority and, in a last-ditch attempt to consolidate the Imperial forces, Admiral Kiril Bloodstar commandeered the Angels' Palace as his central command headquarters. Thanks to the Admiral's brilliant strategy, the Emperor and his family – and the entire Empire – were saved. In gratitude, Stanley One renamed the Angels' Palace and gave it in perpetuity to the Admiral's family, in addition to the unique hereditary title, 'Lord (or Lady) Bloodstar of Bloodstar Hall.'

The Bloodstar family had served the Empire with distinction ever since. They had produced any number of fine statesmen and military officers, and there was seldom a time when a Bloodstar was not a member of the Imperial Council. There had even been Bloodstar marriages into the Stanley line itself, so that the current Lady Bloodstar was number ten in line of succession to the Throne.

Bloodstar Hall, meanwhile, had become the traditional site for all Imperial ceremonies of note. Here was where all Stanley emperors and empresses were crowned; here was where weddings of state occurred, and here was where the Stanleys were mourned when they died. Bloodstar Hall was on the list of any tourist coming to Earth as one of the first places to visit.

The north wing of the hall had been renovated centuries ago into the official residence of the Bloodstar family itself. Thus, though the crowds that had flocked to Earth for Princess Edna's wedding celebration had begun gathering round Bloodstar Hall the day before the ceremony, the north wing was kept free of crowds. The robot duplicate of the current Lady Bloodstar had no problem passing through the cordon of guards the night before the wedding; if anyone had even questioned her being out at that hour, she would have said she'd gone out for a brief walk because she was nervous about the next day's activities.

Once inside the hall, she proceeded straight to 'her' room, where she confronted the real Lady Bloodstar – and that poor woman didn't stand a chance against a robot double who could think and act many times faster than she could, and had incredible mechanical strength besides.

With no one now left to challenge her identity, the robot

mpostor traveled around the hall inspecting the security arrangements. No one would question so important a personage; after all, she had every right to inquire whether the Princess would be safe in this hall tomorrow while theoretically under her protection. Everywhere the robot went outside the hall she left a small timed cannister of TCN-14. Inside the hall, she cached a series of handweapons in predetermined locations. When she finished her inspection, she made a surreptitious trip down to the communications room and sabotaged the incoming lines. No matter how desperately anyone outside the hall tried to call in tomorrow, these lines would look perfectly clear and open. The conspiracy was taking no chances that anyone might accidentally learn of their plans and call in a warning.

The robot's next move was to place a call to a certain vidicom number. She let the receiver at the other end buzz twice, then hung up and called again. This time she only let it buzz once. This was the code signal by which Lady A would know that the hall had been secured, and that all was in readiness for tomorrow's operation.

With that accomplished, the fake aristocrat returned once more to her room. Being a robot, she had no need of sleep, but she lay on the bed with her eyes closed anyway, in case some servant should look in. And as she lay still, she contemplated her orders for the coup tomorrow.

Jules was fuming as he drove through the crowded surface streets in a desperate attempt to reach Bloodstar Hall before the designated hour. He would have loved to let his car open up and fly to the hall, but he was unable to contact the SOTE contingent there – as Lady A had said, the conspiracy had managed to put a blanket on the communications network leading into the hall. Jules knew that any flying craft approaching that hall today without giving warning would be fired on instantly by the Service personnel on duty – and he was in no mood to be shot down by his own side at this stage of the game.

So he drove through crowded streets that had banners flying in celebration of the Princess's wedding; and as he drove he kept hoping beyond hope that he'd be able to prevent it from becoming the occasion of a funeral as well.

The nearer they got to Bloodstar Hall the worse the traffic became, until finally it reached such a point that Jules disgustedly turned off the motor and got out of the car. 'Come on,' he said to Vonnie, 'we can walk faster from here.'

Urgently they pushed their way through the milling throngs, and they were not in the least bit hesitant about using their full DesPlainian strength to shove people aside. When the lives of the Imperial family were at stake, rudeness was an acceptable price to pay.

By the time they had reached the outer gates of the hall they knew their behavior had been noted. The guards posted around the perimeter of the building had been specially alert for anything out of the ordinary, and they'd been picked well. Guns were currently being trained on the Des-Plainian pair, and Jules knew full well they'd be used if he and Vonnie could not explain themselves satisfactorily.

'Keep that enthusiasm under control down there,' one of the guards advised him sternly.

Jules was deeply out of breath, but he managed to call out, 'Wombat: Situation 39!'

All the Service guards froze at their posts for a second. The code name Wombat (Jules) – along with Periwinkle (Yvette) – was almost legendary within the Service. Though the identities of those two super agents were kept well secret, everyone in the Service knew it would cost him his job to disobey an order given by either of those two. In addition, the code phrase 'Situation 39' indicated a crisis on the Imperial level. Either of those code phrases would have been enough to make the leader of the security team spring into instant action; both together made his cooperation imperative.

Beckoning Jules and Vonnie forward, he helped them up into his elevated lookout post. 'Major Mbente at your service, sir. What's wrong?'

'Everything. Is there any way you can communicate into the building?'

Major Mbente punched a button on the console before him and waited. After a moment he gave the board a perplexed look and tried again. There was still no reaction. 'Something seems to be out, sir,' he reported.

Jules grimaced. '*Khorosho*, then here's what you'd better do. Get all your people into gas masks at once. Then clear the streets completely – there are ten cannisters of TCN-14 scattered around the building, and they're due to go off in,' he checked his watch, 'about twenty minutes, at a minute past noon. Don't let the people panic; there's an assassin inside the building, and we don't want to scare her into premature action. Is there any way I can get into the hall?'

'You might try that door over there.'

'*Merci. And get these people away!*'

'Yes sir.' Major Mbente gulped at the enormity of the task. There were upwards of a million people jammed around the perimeter of Bloodstar Hall, with barely a hundred SOTE personnel and three thousand police to control them. Pushing that many people back without giving them the true reason – which would set off a panic – would be an almost impossible job. SOTE agents take pride in accomplishing the impossible, though; so instead of contemplating just how hard the job was, Major Mbente set about grimly relaying instructions to the other lookout posts.

Jules and Vonnie, meanwhile, slipped into the hall through the indicated door. The conditions they found inside would have made Bedlam look like a place of peace and contentment. People were running around behind the scenes, pushing and shoving at one another in mad confusion. At first, Jules feared they were too late and the assassination had already happened; then he realized that all this confusion was just routine for such high state events, with people going crazy in the wings to make everything seem normal out front. He looked about him, but could see no sign of any official SOTE station.

Vonnie was moving ahead of him, elbows swinging viciously as she pushed people out of her way. Even so, the floor area of Bloodstar Hall comprised several square city blocks, all of them jammed with nobility. Squeezing through that mass of humanity to reach the Princess in the short amount of time left would be a nearly impossible task.

When a d'Alembert could not see a way through a problem, he found a way around it. Looking about the immense hall, which could be compared to a larger version of the circus tent under which he'd worked for so many years, Jules had an idea. 'You try to get through on the ground,' he told Vonnie, having to yell to make himself heard above the backstage tumult. 'I'll try another route.'

He elbowed his way to a door marked 'Maintenance' and, to his relief, found it unlocked. Inside was a narrow service corridor that led to, among other things, an elevator tube that could carry workmen to the upper reaches of the hall. He punched a setting for the topmost level and stepped inside. A cushion of air solidified beneath his feet, whisking him upward at a speed that normally would have seemed quite fast. Today, however, nothing moved fast enough to suit him.

He stepped out of the tube to find himself in a world of girders, cables, ropes and pulleys – the superstructure for the roof of Bloodstar Hall. There were catwalks around the perimeter of the roof for the safety of the workmen, but Jules of necessity scorned them. He hadn't come up here to be safe, he'd come because there were no crowds up here, nothing to prevent him from reaching the center of the hall in the fastest time possible.

Leaping over the guide rail he ran along the naked girders that supported the roof, trusting to his aerialist's sense of balance to keep him from falling. He tried not to think of the drop that awaited him if he slipped. Like all natives of high-grav worlds, DesPlainians had an inbred fear of falling. Performers in the Circus of the Galaxy had had that fear trained out of them since childhood, to the point where Jules would think nothing of working even forty meters above the circus ring. Bloodstar Hall, however was built on a bigger scale than that: the floor was a full one hundred meters below him, a drop of approximately thirty stories.

On the floor of the hall, the ceremony had proceeded so far without a hitch. There had been interminable processions all morning as the thousands of visiting nobles, clad in formal Court robes, had marched into the hall according to their rank, preceded by banners, fanfares and all the other pomp of their station. The Imperial Choir had treated the audience to a truly inspirational set of *a capella* renditions. The Imperial Color Guard had given a show of precision drill work and the official bands of many individual Sectors and planets had also paraded around the floor entertaining the waiting audience. Finally, only ten minutes ago, the Emperor and Empress had arrived at their special box, accompanied by their retinue; both were in their full state Court robes, his of scarlet, hers of peacock blue. They bore their massive platinum state crowns with imposing majesty. All festivities had ground to a halt while the royal couple were given a standing ovation lasting seven minutes.

Jules reached the center of the roof structure and looked down. All attention was on the floor as Choyen Liu, the bridegroom from Anares, had just entered from a side aisle with his honor guards. Liu was wearing an undertunic of green, peacock blue and silver brocade; his peacock blue velvet tunic and trousers were cut in Chinese style, lined with silver sable and trimmed with emeralds. On his head, a peacock blue Tibetan crown covered an undercap of emerald green velvet; at his neck, a double set of emerald frogs clasped the tunic together. His peacock blue gloves were heavily jeweled, and a pair of silver leather boots completed his outfit. He looked every centimeter a fit consort for the Galaxy's next ruler.

Jules checked his watch. Eight minutes to go. Soon Princess Edna would be entering from the far end, with the ersatz Lady Bloodstar as her matron-of-honor. He had come this far just by his hunch that it would be the fastest way to go. Now that he was here, he would have to devise some plan for getting down to the action – and quickly.

Although Bloodstar Hall was no longer used as a site for sporting events, the large scoreboard that used to hang from the center of the ceiling was still in existence, pulled up near the top and dangling just fifteen meters below him. The hall was still occasionally used to stage plays and operas, and farther down were ropes from which scenery flats could be raised and lowered. *There should be some way, he thought, for an enterprising young man to use those facts to his advantage. All it takes is a system to get from here to there to there.*

The column that held up the scoreboard was massive,

though small in relation to the scoreboard itself. Wrapping his arms as far around it as he could, Jules slid downward until he was standing atop the giant scoreboard structure. It was big enough to support his weight easily – it had been built to hold several workmen at a time, if need be, for repairs.

As Jules began searching for his next step there was a fanfare below him and the organ music swelled. All heads, including Jules's, turned to the far end of the hall, where Princess Edna had made her entrance.

Edna Stanley was not an excessively beautiful woman, but there was a presence about her that carried her beyond the normal meanings of the word 'beauty'. Though several years younger than Jules, she had spent all her life training to be the next ruler of the Empire of Earth. All the majesty, all the power that went with her future position radiated from her in waves as she stood in the doorway, acknowledging the cheers and applause of this immense crowd.

The Crown Princess was clad in a tightly fitted strapless gown of white satin, heavily embroidered in pearls and diamonds. The overgown of silver spiderweb lace had its cuffs and hemlines heavily trimmed with bands of emeralds and sapphires. She wore a collar of emeralds, with one large square-cut emerald dangling from it as a short pendant. Her headdress was a pagoda-like crown of platinum and diamonds, from which hung emeralds cut into the shape of bells. Her veil was of silver gauze, and reached halfway down her back.

As she walked into the hall, her retinue of attendants followed her. These ladies, noblewomen all, were wearing pastel silk Mandarin court robes, all heavily embroidered, Lady Bloodstar was among them, looking perfectly innocent of any taint of treason.

The time for niceties had passed. Jules could not afford to waste so much as a single second more looking for the safest or most efficient way down. Much as he hated to do it, he would have to come swashbuckling into the middle of the Princess's wedding, making a spectacle of the occasion. He consoled himself with the thought that the alternative was far worse.

The Princess stopped halfway down the aisle, in front of

the Imperial box. At this point her father – a tall, distinguished man with graying hair and regal posture – stepped out beside her and led her the rest of the way down the aisle.

At the same time, Jules leaped from his safe platform downward toward the ropes that were tied back out of the way. It was perhaps the mightiest leap of his life, born entirely of desperation. No man native to Earth would have believed it possible; even Jules himself in a saner moment might not have attempted it, for the alternative if he missed would be a long fall and a horrible crash to the floor below.

Jules used every trick he knew as the premier aerialist of the Galaxy to gain the few extra centimeters he heeded. He flattened his body against the almost unnoticeable air currents circulating in the upper reaches of the hall, stretching his muscles to their utmost in his attempt to reach those ropes. It was the finest single acrobatic performance of his entire life – and it went completely unwitnessed, as everyone within the hall was still watching the Princess and the Emperor making their stately way to the dais.

Jules's fingers tightened on the rope and he pulled himself against it. A surge of relief swept through his body. The impossible had been accomplished. From now on, the rest of what he had to do was almost child's play by comparison. Almost ...

The rope had been tied loosely out of the way, but it had not been intended to hold against the drag of his hundred kilo body. The rope pulled free of its moorings and began a slow pendulum swing out over the audience. This was exactly what Jules had hoped for. At the same time as the rope began its swing, Jules began sliding down its length as rapidly as he could, trying to time his maneuver so that he'd be as low on the rope as possible by the time it reached the nadir of its arc.

Jules knew from experience that a stun-gun would have absolutely no effect on the treacherous robot masquerading as Lady Bloodstar. It would take a blaster bolt, and it would have to be done with a single clean shot. The robots, he knew, had reflexes that put even a DesPlainian to shame, and if he missed on his first try he would not get a second; the robot would have enough time to kill both the Emperor and the Princess. Even if that were not so, he still dared not miss on his first shot – with so many high-ranking nobles in the audience, random blaster fire would certainly wound or kill someone of great importance.

As his rope swung lower, the audience suddenly became aware of him. Heads turned in his direction to stare, and a muffled gasp arose as everyone wondered what brash and unexpected action was occurring. Could this be an assassination attempt? Where were the guards? Where had this stranger come from and how had he managed to do what he did? These and a dozen other questions shot through people's minds, all entirely too late; the action would be completed before anyone could begin to react.

Among the upturned faces that stared at him in wonder, Jules suddenly noticed one that startled him completely – that of Lady A. She had dared to come to the ceremony right under SOTE's very nose! But then, only five people in the entire government knew of her existence – and they had taken great pains that she would remain unaware of the fact. It was only natural that she felt perfectly safe here.

Had Jules known all the grief that lay in store because of that one person, he might have directed his blaster beam at her instead, thereby saving countless lives. But there were only two lives on his mind at the moment – those of the Emperor and the Princess. Both were in imminent peril from the robot, and it was his sworn duty to protect them. With intense concentration, Jules brought all his attention to focus on the figure of Lady Bloodstar, who was standing behind and slightly to the right of the Emperor and Princess. Already the robot had seen Jules coming; her computer-fast brain had analyzed the situation and her right hand was lifting ominously ...

Jules could wait no longer. Even though he was not quite at the bottom of his swing, his hand was a blur of motion as he brought up his blaster and fired. The searing beam streaked out of the nozzle of his gun and raked across the body of the mechanical assassin. Sparks flew, and there was a slight hissing of molten metal and plastic.

Events followed in rapid succession. The Emperor, belatedly recognizing Jules, moved sideways to get out of the line of fire and to knock his beloved daughter to the ground. He covered her with his own body so that if there were any more gunplay at least the Succession would be assured. There was a small explosion from the robot, causing a few minor injuries to nearby spectators but no major catastrophe. The crowd began to shriek in earnest now, convinced that an all-out war was about to erupt.

As Jules's rope reached bottom and started to rise again, he let go and allowed his momentum to carry him soaring out over the crowd. Twisting in midair, he again sought Lady A. He caught a quick glance of her, but the beautiful conspirator had managed to duck down within a group of bystanders who had risen to their feet in panic. Jules could not get a clear shot at her and he refused to shoot wildly with his blaster into this crowd.

Jules had enough control over his flight to be able to land in a relatively empty spot. He knocked over a handful of people as he bowled into them and rolled awkwardly to his feet again. If he couldn't shoot Lady A from the air, he would pursue her on foot; he was determined to capture her this time. Fate, however, conspired against him.

Suddenly there was gunplay from several points around the hall, and Jules looked about in confusion. He hadn't known there were any accomplices scattered around, but they were certainly a menace to be dealt with. Even as he got to his feet, he found himself staring down the barrel of a stun-gun. Before he could raise his own weapon in defense, the person threatening him sank to the floor, unconscious – and looking beyond, Jules could see Duchess Helena von Wilmenhorst, decked out in her finest formal gown and holding a ministunner in her hand. She smiled at Jules, then turned to look for more targets around the hall.

Vonnie, too, was making her presence felt throughout the chamber. She had relaxed slightly when she saw Jules take care of the menace from the robot, but when the shooting erupted elsewhere she rose instantly to the challenge. Two would-be terrorists fell before they could even get their guns clear of their holsters, and three more did but minimal damage before succumbing to Vonnie's attack.

Panic was now endemic throughout the audience, and spectators were rushing headlong for the exits. Jules and

Vonnie noted that flight with dismay. They had warned Major Mbente outside to clear the crowds away from the hall so that the TCN-14 would not harm anyone – and now more people were going outside to be threatened by the deadly gas.

They were not taking into account, however, the resourcefulness of Major Mbente. Realizing that completely clearing the streets would have been an impossible task, he opted for the other alternative: finding and containing the cannisters of TCN-14 that had been planted. Working against time and without the proper equipment, the major and his people still managed to conduct an inspection of the area so thoroughly that all ten cannisters were found and removed to a place of safety before they could explode and send their lethal contents throughout the crowd that surrounded Bloodstar Hall. The emergence a few minutes later of the panicked people from inside the hall was a serious complication, but not a fatal one.

Inside, the forces of SOTE were once again asserting their authority. The Head had hand-picked the security teams to work within the hall, and his faith in them was proving justified. Despite the crush of people in the immense building, the threat from the terrorists was over five minutes after it had begun.

As the Head came over to him to both congratulate him and lead him into a quiet area for further questioning, Jules looked around the hall, discouraged. The threat from the robot had been ended, and even the unexpected uprising of the terrorists had been quelled. But Lady A, whom he had hoped to capture, had vanished without a trace into the milling mob.

CHAPTER THIRTEEN

THE WEDDING OF THE GALAXY

By the time the subcom call from Yvette at the pirate base came through to the Head on Earth, the attempted coup and assassination were all over but the final shouting. Her story of the people impersonating the nobles who'd been aboard the *Querida* came too late to serve as a warning, but it did function nicely as an explanation for the sudden burst of terrorist activities from a supposedly safe and friendly audience. Yvette closed by saying that she, Pias and Duke Etienne would be speeding back to Earth at once to give a personal report. Traveling at top speed, they expected to arrive in a couple of days.

The decision was made to postpone the actual wedding for a few more days, as well. Princess Edna, while trying to project an impression of imperial calm, was inwardly shaken by her close call and the startling events of what she'd expected to be the happiest day of her life. Choyen Liu was comforting her by holding her tightly and quoting soothing passages from Anares's mystical books; he seemed as totally unflappable as ever, and his inward peace was a blessing to everyone. It was reassuring to know that the man who would be sharing the Throne with the Galaxy's future ruler could remain so serene even under such trying circumstances.

The days following the fighting at Bloodstar Hall were almost as busy for Jules and Vonnie as the ones that preceded it. The pirate doubles knew no organizational details of the conspiracy for which they were working. The gangsters, at Jules's orders, were picked up by SOTE from the hospital where they'd been taken after the fire fighters found them unconscious in Howard's gym. Most of them were just hired blasterbats, and knew nothing about higher operations within the conspiracy. Howard, however, was a fount of knowledge on Earthly crime, and it took surprisingly little coercion to make him reveal everything he knew on a variety of subjects.

The vidicom number and address he had for Lady A turned out to be a suite of offices in one of Angeles–Diego's classier office buildings. The suite had been rented to a woman obviously fitting the description of Lady A; she had operated under the name 'Sarah Schmidt', and had paid cash in advance for everything. The office had only been rented up until the day of the wedding. 'Obviously she figured she wouldn't need it after that,' Jules surmised. 'If her plan failed, she'd want to be gone in a hurry – and if it succeeded, she could be living in the Imperial Palace after that date.'

'Sarah Schmidt' had, of course, vanished without a trace, leaving Jules and the Head as frustrated as ever in their attempts to track down her conspiracy.

When Yvette's party arrived, the Head called a council of war. In attendance were he and his daughter Helena, Jules, Yvette and Duke Etienne. The elder d'Alembert had not seen the Grand Duke in person for over five years, and their reunion was a friendly one, with much hugging and backslapping.

When everyone was settled, the Head took some time to acquaint Duke Etienne with what was known about Lady A and her conspiracy. 'Some of the pressure of secrecy is off us now,' he said. 'After the attempted coup and our capturing and questioning Howard, the enemy *knows* we know about them; for us to pretend not to would look suspicious. SOTE is now officially aware that Lady A exists, and that she is a powerful and high-ranking officer in an organization dedicated to the overthrow of the Stanley dynasty. Period. They still don't know we're aware of their boast that they know most of what's going on within the Service – and our keeping them from knowing that may lead them into the trap of overconfidence. I'm still convinced they know nothing about the Circus's role, nor about the true identities of agents Wombat and Periwinkle; if they did, they'd be conducting their campaign in an entirely different manner from the way they are.'

The Head sighed. 'Secrets within secrets within secrets. It makes it hard for all of us, but we have to play within those rules when the stakes are as high as the safety of the Empire. There are days I'd like to chuck the whole thing and go back to tending my garden at home...'

He let the thought drift off. Everyone in the room knew

154

the burden of duty, and each of them had at one time or another harbored similar dreams of freedom. But they all knew how impossible those dreams would be; their own inward sense of responsibility made them the people they were.

The Head derailed that train of thought quickly. 'Be that as it may,' he said, 'I believe Yvette has another piece of the puzzle for us.'

Yvette briefed everyone on the conversation she and Pias had overheard at the pirate base, and about the new figure in the picture: C. 'They seem to have an inordinate fondness for letters of the alphabet,' she finished cynically.

'One piece of nonsense is as good as another for covering true identities,' the Head commented. 'It makes just as much sense to use the alphabet as it does for us to call you two by the names of rather esoteric terrestrial organisms. The question is, how much do we "officially" know about C?'

'Nothing,' Yvette said. 'Both Ling and the man who brought him that message died in the battle with our people. None of the other pirates seems to know anything about him.'

'Which gives us one more secret to work with,' the Head said. 'Let me remind you all again: officially, we know that Lady A exists, and we have pictures of her taken by Vonnie during her surveillance of Howard. We'll be actively looking for her now, too. Believe me.'

'What I don't understand,' Duke Etienne said, 'is how those impostors managed to sneak their guns into the hall. Were you falling down on the job, Zan?'

'Our arrangements were adequate for what we thought was the situation,' Helena snapped, a little upset at having her father accused so familiarly. 'Every guest was screened discreetly as he went in. Nobody but our people carried a weapon past the front door.'

'We should at least have the decency to blush,' the Head reminded his daughter. 'We should have anticipated a little better. We've learned from questioning some of the terrorists that a confederate – probably the robot Lady Bloodstar – left their weapons in prearranged spots so that while they came in clean, they could arm themselves inside the hall. I *am* proud, however, of the way our people handled the problem once it broke out. Operating under those conditions, I think we did a superb job, and everyone on the security team, inside and out, has received a special commendation.

'The thing that worries me more than the guns, though, is the question of their identities. Even given the fact that they had perfectly forged IDs, they still should not have been able to wander around on Earth for two days without a discrepancy showing up in our files somewhere. I'm most *un*happy about that, and I intend to see that there's a shakeup in the Computer Correlation department because of it.'

From that point, the conversation devolved into a discussion of more general topics – including weddings. It had been decided that there was no need to repeat the lavish ceremony of Princess Edna's wedding; the festivities had been rescheduled for tomorrow afternoon and would be conducted in relative privacy, though the ceremony would be vidicast all over the Empire. Edna had been disappointed before that her friends Jules and Yvette would be working and unable to attend the festivities; now that they were both here, she insisted that they both be present, and they were happy enough to agree.

And while the subject of weddings was in the air, they decided that two more should take place at the same time – the marriage of Jules and Vonnie and the marriage of Pias and Yvette. The Emperor himself insisted on officiating at those two ceremonies, which set the young people blushing furiously. Yvette and Helena excused themselves at that point saying that they had to round up Vonnie and get a lot of pre-wedding shopping done in just one day.

Everyone was nervous the next day as they gathered in the Grand Ballroom of the Imperial Palace. Princess Edna and Choyen Liu were wearing the wedding outfits they'd worn at the official ceremony, cleaned and repaired after the harsh abuse they'd received a few days earlier.

Yvette and Pias were both in outfits of red and gold. Under normal Newforest tradition, Pias would have worn a wedding shirt embroidered by his mother – but that shirt had been burned when his family disowned him. Instead, he wore a cloth-of-gold shirt embroidered in red with red velvet pants and an open red velvet vest. A large ruby hung in the center of his chest, suspended by a gold chain. He wore red leather boots and a full length red velvet cape with a high flared collar; the entire cape was lined with cloth-of-gold. In his right hand he carried a single red rose.

Yvette wore a cloth-of-gold gauze peasant shirt, a red velvet vest laced up the front, and a tiered skirt of red and gold silk brocade. She had a red silk scarf on her hair, red velvet slippers on her feet and a string of rubies around her neck. In the crook of her left arm was nestled a full bouquet of red roses.

Her brother Jules was clad in a gold acrobat's jumpsuit heavily embroidered in pearls and diamonds. His gold belt was trimmed with rubies, his gold chaplet was set with a ruby in the center, while still another large ruby dangled as a pendant from his gold collar. He wore a white satin cape, white pearl-embroidered gloves and white embroidered boots.

Vonnie, meanwhile, looked ravishing in an ivory satin gown cut like an acrobat's robe; the shawl collar hemline and sleeves were all thickly embroidered with pearls, and her belt was a chain of pearls with pearl-cluster tassels. She wore a pearl necklace and ivory satin slippers. On her head was a crown of pearls set on thin wire springs that moved when her head moved. As with Yvette, she carried a bouquet of roses, but Vonnie's were yellow rather than red.

This was the first time Jules had seen Edna since the fiasco on Saturday, and he approached her rather sheepishly. 'I have to apologize for messing things up the way I did,' he said. 'If I'd been a little more on the ball, I could probably have saved you a lot of embarrassment.'

Edna kissed him lightly on the cheek. 'I'd rather be embarrassed than dead. And the way I see it, you saved me from more than just an assassin – you also saved me from having to spend at least six boring hours on a receiving line. For that alone you deserve a medal.'

The royal wedding, though lacking some of the grandeur of the previous attempt, was a beautiful production none the less. Barr, the imperial bard, sang a wedding march of his own composition that was a work of pure inspiration.

The ceremony went off without so much as a single mistake this time, and the scene vidcast to homes all across the Empire was one of unrestrained happiness. The SOTE agents, of course, stayed well out of camera range — it would never do to have their faces broadcast all over the Galaxy.

After the major ceremony, the celebrants retired to a more private room for the two weddings that were less public in nature. Though the guest list was small, it was impressive: Duke Etienne, in a scarlet velvet jumpsuit, a short, Spanish-style coat of black velvet embroidered in gold and a boutonnière of a red and yellow rose, gave both brides away, in his capacity as Yvette's father and as a close friend of Vonnie's father, Baron Ebert Roumenier; Crown Princess Edna served as matron-of-honor for Yvette, while the Empress Irene served in that capacity for Vonnie; and true to his word, His Imperial Majesty William Stanley, the supreme temporal authority in the Galaxy, pronounced the words that united the two couples in the bonds of matrimony.

In the general revelries that followed the ceremonies, Vonnie noticed a certain preoccupation on the part of her new husband. When she questioned him about it, he said, 'I just can't help but feel a little guilty that I let Lady A escape when I had the chance to catch her.'

The Emperor overheard his remark, and leaned over to give him some advice. 'Young man, Lady A and her nefarious deeds will wait a little while. I order you to forget her and enjoy yourself.'

'Besides,' Vonnie said, 'if I catch you thinking about another woman on *our* wedding night, you won't survive the honeymoon. That's a promise!'

Since it is a recorded fact that Jules d'Alembert survived his honeymoon, we may therefore safely assume that Vonnie did keep his mind off Lady A — at least for a while.

The world's greatest science fiction authors now available in Panther Books

Ray Bradbury

Fahrenheit 451	£1.25	☐
The Small Assassin	£1.50	☐
The October Country	£1.25	☐
The Illustrated Man	£1.50	☐
The Martian Chronicles	£1.50	☐
Dandelion Wine	£1.50	☐
The Golden Apples of the Sun	£1.50	☐
Something Wicked This Way Comes	£1.50	☐
The Machineries of Joy	£1.50	☐
Long After Midnight	£1.50	☐
The Stories of Ray Bradbury (Volume 1)	£2.95	☐
The Stories of Ray Bradbury (Volume 2)	£2.95	☐

Philip K Dick

Flow my Tears, The Policeman Said	£1.95	☐
Blade Runner (Do Androids Dream of Electric Sheep?)	£1.75	☐
Now Wait for Last Year	£1.50	☐
The Zap Gun	75p	☐
A Handful of Darkness	£1.50	☐

To order direct from the publisher just tick the titles you want and fill in the order form.

All these books are available at your local bookshop or newsagent, or can be ordered direct from the publisher..

To order direct from the publisher just tick the titles you want and fill in the form below.

Name_____

Address _____

_____

Send to:
Panther Cash Sales
PO Box 11, Falmouth, Cornwall TR10 9EN.

Please enclose remittance to the value of the cover price plus:

UK 45p for the first book, 20p for the second book plus 14p per copy for each additional book ordered to a maximum charge of £1.63.

BFPO and Eire 45p for the first book, 20p for the second book plus 14p per copy for the next 7 books, thereafter 8p per book.

Overseas 75p for the first book and 21p for each additional book.

Panther Books reserve the right to show new retail prices on covers, which may differ from those previously advertised in the text or elsewhere